A BAKER STREET MYSTERY

## THE CASE OF

# THE MALTESE TREASURE

### Thomas Brace Haughey

**Bethany Fellowship** INC.
MINNEAPOLIS, MINNESOTA 55438

*The Case of the Maltese Treasure*
Thomas Brace Haughey

Library of Congress Catalog Card Number 79-54939

ISBN 0-87123-048-8

Copyright © 1979
Thomas Brace Haughey
All Rights Reserved

Published by Bethany Fellowship, Inc.
6820 Auto Club Road, Minneapolis, Minnesota 55438

Printed in the United States of America

## *Dedication*

To the pioneer undersea explorer, Vincent Palmer, whose suggestions proved invaluable, and to my two-year-old daughter, Dawn, who specializes in smiles and sabotage.

THOMAS BRACE HAUGHEY is the General Director of The Evangelical Latin League Mission and its branch, Fireside Productions. He is also involved in the work of missionary radio station KVMV-FM in McAllen, Texas. He received his bachelor's degree from the University of Maryland in 1965, and a Th.M. from Capital Bible Seminary in 1969. In addition, he received a diploma from Rio Grande Bible Institute Language School. While at the University of Maryland, he was inducted into the literary honorary society, Phi Delta Epsilon. He has done evangelism and youth work in Mexico, and taught for a year and a half in a missionary Bible school. His experience as a writer includes: Editing a Jesus Paper, writing numerous articles, writing scripts for "Folk Festival," a weekly radio program, and more than 100 book reviews each year for broadcast. His first two books are *The Case of the Invisible Thief* and *The Case of the Frozen Scream*, published by Bethany Fellowship, Inc., in 1978 and 1979, respectively. Mr. Haughey is married, has one daughter, and makes his home in McAllen, Texas.

# *Preface*

Francois-Eugene Vidocq could scarcely have realized his full impact on the world when he founded the first detective bureau back in 1817. His Paris office became the pattern for today's modern police force. It also provided the spark for an entirely new and exciting form of literature—the mystery story. Since the time of Vidocq over ten thousand writers—mostly from the West—have taken pen in hand to chronicle the exploits of their favorite sleuths. The whodunit has become, in fact, a major trademark of our free society. Wherever the police are viewed as instruments of justice rather than of oppression, readers have embraced detectives and welcomed them as heroes.

Our culture, perhaps, needs heroes. Corporations have grown bigger and bigger until the individual seems rather insignificant. And a nine-to-five routine squeezes us into a mold. What a welcome relief to be able to pick up a detective novel and escape into a world without time clocks where one or two imperfect individualists battle impossible odds and find truth! The mystery story echoes the aspirations of the common man. The crime fighter is someone with whom we can all relate.

Geoffrey Weston is a case in point. He's not particularly handsome, dresses very casually, and has been known to lose his temper a time or two. Does that sound familiar? In addition, he more closely resembles a basketball player than a sleuth. But underneath that unlikely exterior lurks one of the keenest minds ever to enter the fray against lawlessness. When not cooking delicacies or causing dire pain to his partner with a well-placed pun, Weston immerses himself in the tireless pursuit of thieves and murderers.

One of the things I personally like about Geoff is his uncanny knack for devastating opponents in debate. You and I might answer lamely and then ten minutes later snap our fingers and say, "I wish I'd said that!" Geoffrey actually says it! He also has—and this is unusual for a detective—a deep sense of compassion. Both the compassion and the flair for rhetoric probably find their roots in his commitment to Christ. Weston is, you see, a Christian. Some years ago he investigated the mystery of the cross, found himself guilty, and accepted a pardon. That mystery solved the detective.

In his latest investigation, Geoffrey Weston and his partner John Taylor, Esq., look into a series of crimes so baffling that even they despair of an answer. What possible connection could a diver's death off the coast of Malta have with a more recent jewel robbery in London? How could a thief steal diamonds from a *sealed* fortress when he himself was caught inside? As the plot thickens, one of Weston's own theories threatens to convict what may well be an innocent man. If you'd like a taste of adventure—and who wouldn't—then turn the page and join with the two detectives as they try to solve *The Case of the Maltese Treasure*.

# Contents

CHAPTER 1 — Puff Go the Diamonds! ..... 11

CHAPTER 2 — Who Cased the Case? ....... 23

CHAPTER 3 — Ersatz Wisdom ........... 44

CHAPTER 4 — Lumps ................... 69

CHAPTER 5 — The Breathless Grin ........ 91

CHAPTER 6 — The Island Fortress ........118

CHAPTER 7 — The Hidden Reef ..........133

EPILOGUE ...........................157

# CHAPTER 1

## *Puff Go the Diamonds!*

Our brownstone's shadow had lengthened and now extended across Baker Street. But a hound being taken for its afternoon stroll still pranced on the hot sidewalk. The city was baked in the kiln of August—an August so fierce that gardens had turned to brown skeletons and London bookies were swamped with bets on when the next drop of rain would fall.

Our living-room window, along with everyone else's, was slung open in hopes of catching a breeze. But the air outside hung heavy and still. Inside only the methodical whirring of a fan managed to redistribute the mugginess. This was suicide weather—a month of flairing tempers, murder, and despair. My own spirits, however, were anything but downcast. With two tickets to the symphony in my pocket, I didn't even grumble as a starched collar did its best to strangle me. I fumbled with my bow tie but failed once again to get the loops right. If only there were a mirror handy! My colleague, Geoffrey Weston, looked up from grinding a lens in our "laboratory corner" and gazed at me across ten feet of casual disorder. He wiped carborundum paste off his hands and shook his head sympathetically.

"John, sitting here with my shirttail out I'm in no position to criticize. And you know I don't wear tuxedos. They make a chap as tall and thin as I look like an undertaker. But don't you think you should make a few changes? Miss Albey is likely to mistake you tonight for some overstuffed toy sporting a Christmas ribbon. At the very least go rent a suit that fits. There should be a shoppe still open somewhere. And please buy yourself one of those pre-tied, clip-on bows. As much as I hate the things, they do have the advantage of not drooping."

I breathed in to take the strain off protesting buttons.

"This suit," I informed Weston gravely, "was good enough to wear for an audience with the King. And it shall afford many more years of service. It's a mite cozy right now, I'll grant you. But it shall not remain so."

Geoffrey smiled at my wishful thinking and held the lens up to the light to inspect its polish. He looked like some goateed jeweler searching for an imperfection in the Star of India. But I had the uneasy feeling that he was weighing his next words—or to be more precise, that I was being weighed in the balances and found three stone overweight. Just then Gladstone meowed plaintively at the front door. Grateful for the interruption, I walked over to let our pet in before he clawed the screen to shreds. When I pushed the door open, however, the rascal's eagerness vanished. He looked up at me in perfect boredom. I could almost hear him thinking, "It's about time you got here. You're not very well trained yet." With deliberate slowness he took a last lick at his long, white fur and strolled disinterestedly through the doorway. I was about to close the screen and turn away when I noticed a very agitated, elderly gentleman approaching the front gate. In spite of the heat the fellow was wearing a bowler hat. His eyes were close set. And by the stylish yet conservative cut of his suit I judged he was straight out of some financial establishment. Without so much as glancing in my direction, he began violently shaking the wrought iron barrier. I stepped forward, as much out of curiosity as from a desire to be seen, and shouted over the din.

"Hold on a minute there, mate. You'll arouse the neighborhood with that clanging. What do you want, anyway?"

He jerked his hands from the bars as though caught in an indiscretion.

"Dreadfully sorry!" His high, clipped voice betrayed near hysteria. "MY GOOD MAN, why on earth aren't you listed in the telephone directory? I've already wasted twenty minutes coming here. Please show me in to see the detective AT ONCE."

In answer I reached back inside the building

and pushed the button that unlatched the gate. By the time I could turn around again our caller had scurried up the walk and stood nose to nose with me. He was like some racer with engine running awaiting the starter's shot. I was the obstacle that barred his way. Almost in self-defense my hand came up and grasped his in a firm greeting.

"It's good to meet you, sir," I assured him calmly. "But I'm afraid I'm neither a butler nor a gentleman's gentleman. My goodness is also rather debatable. Now with which investigator did you wish to speak? There are two of us, you know."

"You're a—"

"Yes, I'm afraid so."

"But you seem—"

"There's no law," I pointed out with a touch of reproach, "that a consulting detective must dress slovenly. John Taylor, Esq. at your service."

He registered relief.

"Then you're not Mr. Weston."

"No. But Geoffrey's inside, and we generally work together. If you'll step this way . . . ."

I didn't have to repeat the invitation. Our visitor brushed past me, strode nervously into the living room, and nearly tripped over Gladstone. The man would have been comical if he weren't so obviously distraught. His head jerked from side to side like a chicken's as he surveyed the surroundings. The resulting scowl spoke volumes. He was decidedly unsatisfied with our housekeeping.

My partner eased his angular frame from behind the work bench and gestured expansively as he came over to join us. His friendliness was unmistakable as he attempted to undo the bad impression.

"As they say in Spain," he remarked pleasantly, " 'it's your house . . .' from that pile of books on the mantle to the dust on the floor. If you rate your sleuths for neatness, I'm afraid we won't do at all. But if you're interested in solving a crime, then you've come to the right office."

Our prospective client studied Geoffrey critically for a second—as though unwilling to admit that a beanpole in a floppy, stained shirt could really be competent.

"So I've heard," he admitted at length. "You come highly recommended. What's your fee?"

Weston, taken somewhat aback by the man's abruptness, replied in kind.

"That depends," he observed, "on whether I'll be representing you or Lloyds."

The chap jumped as though he'd stuck his finger in a light socket.

"How did you know I was. . ."

". . . in the employ of Lloyds of London?" Geoff finished for him—thoroughly enjoying the moment. "I hate to tarnish the mystique by explaining. But your motorcar out front has a parking sticker on its bumper, and I AM polishing telescopic lenses. Now will you please tell us who you are and why you've come."

For the first time since he'd walked through the gate the gentleman lost his domineering attitude. He sighed and suddenly seemed very old.

"You'll have to forgive me, Mr. Weston. I suppose I've been rather curt. But I'm under such pressure." He removed his hat and gripped it in front of him until his knuckles turned white. His voice, when he resumed, quivered slightly.

"I'm only two years away from being a pensioner, you see. But something has happened which may cost me my employment. It's absolutely incredible! And those bumblers at Scotland Yard seem utterly confused. If you don't come immediately they'll let the thief get away."

"Then you're talking about a burglary."

"Yes. But you've never seen anything like it. Guards caught the blighter inside, but the jewels are gone! And I'm the one who approved the security system—only two weeks ago!"

Geoffrey wiped perspiration from his forehead, then gestured by way of invitation toward one of our overstuffed chairs.

"Please be seated Mr. . . . I don't believe you've mentioned your name yet."

"Wiggens. Donald Wiggens."

"Have a seat, Mr. Wiggens. Collect your thoughts and relax. As tense as you are you're likely to leave out important details. And we can't have that."

"But you simply must come right now. They'll turn him loose if we—"

"I'm certain that the Yard will handle matters competently," Geoffrey interrupted. "And I haven't agreed to accept the case as yet."

He put an arm on Wiggens' shoulder and steered him firmly in the desired direction.

"Would you care for something to drink? Some iced tea perhaps or quinine water? On my last trip to the Far East I found that to be particularly refreshing with just a dash of lemon added."

Donald Wiggens resigned himself to his fate and sat down. But his fingers drummed a solo on the arm of the chair.

"I'd prefer tea—without sugar, thank you."

Weston positioned himself across from our guest while I hurried to the kitchen. My trip, as well as the mushy chairs, was a part of our routine. Small talk, comfort, and tea calmed clients and often enabled us to get a clearer picture of a crime. I returned shortly and handed Wiggens his glass. Geoffrey accepted a lemon drink. Then I sank into my own easy chair and looked expectantly at our distinguished visitor. He took a sip of tea and shifted uneasily.

"Mr. Weston, . . . Mr. Taylor, . . . when Lloyds agrees to insure a collection, I am one of the agents the firm sends to advise clients on correct security procedures. And when valuables are moved, I'm called in to approve the new locations. Inadequate protection, as you know, may result in higher rates or in cancellation of a policy."

Geoffrey nodded approvingly.

"Quite so. And you were asked to make such an inspection?"

"Yes. You've no doubt heard about the new annex to the British Museum. It opened to the public only yesterday. And I'd stake my career that it is burglar proof!"

"You evidently have," Geoffrey reminded him. "Would you give us some details on the alarm system?"

"Certainly." Wiggens unconsciously took on the air of an instructor. He seemed more at ease now that he was in his area of specialty. "Every exhibit case is wired so that a bell sounds if the glass is broken. At that time the exit doors also close automatically. They're computer activated."

That last comment seemed rather strange to me.

"Why," I asked, "is a computer necessary? Couldn't a simple electrical relay do the job?"

Donald ran his fingers through his streaky, grey hair and glanced at me with the barely concealed impatience of an expert forced to explain the obvious.

"It could, Mr. Taylor, but that arrangement wouldn't pass the fire inspection. In the event of a blaze or an explosion the glass might crack. And it would hardly do to trap everyone inside. The computer senses smoke and changes in temperature as well as damage to the cases. If an explosion ruptures the glass, the alarm still sounds but the doors remain open."

"I seem to remember," Geoffrey reflected, "that the annex is one of those new energy efficient buildings with earth banked on the outer walls. I take it there are no windows."

"Neither windows nor sky lights. And every

guard has a spotless record and at least ten years of experience! Yet the place was robbed this very afternoon."

My partner leaned forward and fixed a penetrating gaze upon the Lloyds agent.

"Would you please be more precise?" he requested. "What was stolen? When, to the best of your knowledge, did the incident take place? And what was the modus operandi?"

Donald smiled weakly.

"If I knew the answer to that last question, sir, I wouldn't be here. But I'll give you as many particulars as I can." He took out a small note pad and flipped it open to a newly filled page. "Now let me see . . . Shortly after closing time—at exactly ten past six—the bell sounded in the annex and the front doors clanged shut. They're made of brass, you know, and quite solid."

"And the other exits?"

"There are three in all, and they'd already been secured for the night."

"Quite so," Geoffrey remarked with evident satisfaction. "What was the guards' reaction?"

"Well, a display panel in the entrance hall indicated the trouble was in the Queen Victoria Room, so they started off in that direction. But then the fire alarm went off and the men came rushing back to push the override button before the main door opened again."

"Did it?"

"Only a crack." Wiggens paused to sip his iced tea. "And the other doors were, of course, unaffected since they'd already been locked. As a precaution the chief of security then put every exit under guard before leading a contingent to the Victoria Room."

"How long did that take?"

"Not above three minutes. When he arrived he discovered the Queen on fire and two display cases smashed. The entire Weatherford diamond collection was missing!"

"By the Queen," I interrupted, "you mean—"

"A wax dummy dressed in the fashion of the nineteenth century."

Geoffrey stroked his goatee in thought. He seemed impressed by the thief's efficiency but decidedly unimpressed with his manners.

"The robber," he noted coolly, "was not one for patriotism. Most Englishmen would sooner desecrate the union jack than dishonor Her Majesty. Did the guards turn up any clues?"

"They did for a fact," Wiggens scowled. "They caught the billy boy right inside. But now the Yard is going to turn him loose."

"Why on earth would they do that!" I protested.

Our visitor looked pained and spat out his reply.

"Because they can't find the jewels! They've x-rayed the rogue. They're turning the annex upside down. And so far they've come up empty. If you two don't uncover the diamonds, he's going to walk out scot free."

"But surely," Geoffrey reasoned, "they could hold him on a trespassing charge."

"They can, Mr. Weston, but they won't. The liar says he was so engrossed in looking at some paintings that he didn't notice the museum close. And that imbecile Inspector Twigg believes him!"

Our visitor's last words lit a twinkle in Geoff's eye. My partner's face broke into a broad grin and he slapped the arm of the chair decisively.

"Good show, Wiggens! That clinches it. We could never pass up a chance to help out our friend Twigg!" Weston swung to his feet and walked over to the telephone. "John, I'll call the Yard and let them know we're on our way to the museum. It wouldn't do to march in unannounced. And while I'm at it I'll cancel your date with Miss Albey. Grab me a clean shirt, will you. And please get out of that penguin outfit. There's work to do and precious little time in which to do it. We've got to track down those diamonds before they're recut."

By the time I pushed myself out of the chair and hurried down the hall, Geoffrey's finger had already dialed the first set of numbers. I ventured Twigg would be "delighted" to hear of our plans—about as happy as a cobra facing a mongoose. I unpeeled and in best fireman fashion slid into something more comfortable. On the way back I detoured to Geoff's bedroom and snagged a Hawaiian short-sleeved monstrosity from off the bedpost. As I neared the living room my partner's voice rang out impatiently.

"Hurry up there, John. Our briefcase is packed with equipment and arrangements have been made." His tone softened—becoming almost inaudible. "Yes, Mr. Wiggens, that retainer should prove quite satisfactory. I see your address and telephone number are on the cheque. If you'll return home now we will get in touch when you're needed."

I bounded in, tossed my partner his shirt, and relieved him of the valise. As Wiggens led the procession out toward our motorcar, Weston was still struggling to get his arms through wrinkled sleeves.

# CHAPTER 2

## *Who Cased the Case?*

The engine under the bonnet throbbed with controlled power as we made the turn onto Oxford Street and accelerated. Traffic was dense, but Geoffrey handled the Mercedes with the skill of a professional—jockeying for position and catching more than our share of green lights. The sun was now a rosy glow on the horizon. Pedestrians milled about on the sidewalks or sat on steps while engaging in pointless conversation. The evening migration of tenants from sweltering flats had begun. As I watched I silently thanked God that my own life wasn't so aimless.

"What," I wondered aloud, "do you think we'll find at the museum?"

Before answering, Geoffrey jerked the wheel hard to the right and swerved into the center lane.

"I haven't the foggiest," he admitted. "But I know what we won't find. Those diamonds aren't within a mile of the annex."

"You're certain of that?"

My colleague's face remained impassive as he concentrated on the road.

"Reasonably. One can never rule out the possibility of random illogic, of course. But I cannot picture a man being clever enough to hide jewels where the Yard hasn't found them but stupid enough to hide them at all."

"I'm not sure I follow."

"Of course you do," Weston bantered. "Think the matter through. When do you predict the annex will open again to the public?"

I frowned and considered the matter.

"Why I suppose as soon as the gems are recovered or every possible hiding place is eliminated."

"Exactly. The Yard is going to literally tear that building apart. If jewels are there, they'll unearth them. And no confederate is going to amble in as part of Monday's crowd and make off with the booty. Our thief's no fool. He must have determined from the beginning his only chance lay in quickly removing the prize. I conclude, therefore, that he has in fact done so."

"But," I protested, "you're talking about an impossible crime. The place was completely sealed off!"

"So it would seem." My partner grew quiet—savoring the thought.

Our station wagon angled left onto Bloomsbury Way just as the tower bell of St. George's Church chimed. It was eight-thirty. I realized with satisfaction that we would be arriving within three hours of the theft. Clients seldom sought help so promptly and Wiggens' quick action might bring us one or two extra untrampled clues. Geoffrey turned up Bury Place and the columns of the old domed museum came into view. It was a magnificent sight!

We covered the few remaining blocks and maneuvered toward the annex. For once there was plenty of parking space! Our Mercedes rolled to a stop not more than fifty feet from the front entrance. The contrast between the old and the new was striking. Across the street the main building stood stately and unafraid to express the hopes and dreams of its builders. But the floodlit structure directly before us was somehow cold and impersonal—the product of the lowest bid. I was overwhelmed by its massiveness.

"Nice place," Weston observed wryly. "There's one museum that's not going to be a monument. It looks more like a crypt."

"Or a vault," I agreed. "And that makes our own job all the more difficult. Even with earth banked on those walls a second-story man would have a good twenty-foot climb to the roof."

Geoff peered upward with the studied eye of a mountaineer, then nodded.

"A rather slippery climb at that! Polished marble does not lend itself to scaling. And who's to say there's any air duct on top to reward our hypothetical steeple jack. With a building this large a man might be able to slither up it undetected, but . . . "

"The outer doors don't offer any better prospect," I pointed out. "They look to be a good four inches thick. Why is it that museum entrances are always built to accommodate visitors three heads taller than Goliath?"

"That," Geoffrey chuckled, "is one of the great, unanswered questions of our time. What say we toddle on in now and see if we can't solve a few less perplexing puzzles." As he spoke, his hand reached for the door handle.

A few seconds later we were briskly walking up the steps. The annex loomed above awaiting our passage through its brazen jaws. And it was not disappointed. We hurried on into the vestibule. A glass panel slid aside automatically, and we stepped into the empty lobby. There marble gleamed under indirect lighting and onyx statues took turns at trying to look naked or noble. A large illuminated map on the far wall offered us a bird's-eye tour of the establishment. I groaned. There were fifty-two display rooms!

"May I help you, gentlemen?"

We started at the sound and whirled to look behind us. There in a recessed area by the door sat a very smug Inspector Twigg. He had his feet up on a guard's desk, his coat open, and a copy of *Punch* perched on his lap.

"Well, well," he teased, "you're on your toes as usual, I see. Observing everything. Not like those dullards at the Yard." He pushed a button on the wall, and the outer door slowly swung closed.

Geoff took a deep breath before attempting an answer.

"Only flies, old fellow, have eyes in the back of their heads. Since you've taken time off to play games, I assume matters here are pretty much under control."

"You might say that." Twigg tossed the magazine onto the desk and got to his feet. He was only medium height but built like a bulldog. "We are reasonably certain of the thief, and we hope to recover the diamonds by morning."

" 'Reasonably certain . . . hope to,' " I repeated skeptically. "You don't sound overly dogmatic."

"I'll leave the dogmatism to you two," Twigg grimaced. "The force specializes in following leads and in wearing out shoe leather."

"Leads is in Yorkshire," Weston observed dryly. "One would wish you'd found it by now. If you'll be good enough to guide us to the Victoria Room, we can talk about your suspect on the way."

"Certainly," the Inspector agreed. "I'll *lead*. You follow."

I was unable to suppress a groan.

"If puns were a crime," I warned, "you two would be in gaol for life. Will you please stop sniping long enough so we can get to work."

Twigg's face broke into a broad grin. He slapped me soundly on the back and began ushering us toward the center hall. As we walked he filled us in on the day's events.

"Actually, I'm delighted to see you characters again. You're just the thing to liven up a rather boring case. Sorry I haven't been able to drop by for chess lately, but we're working extra shifts during the vacation months."

"Quite all right," Weston acknowledged. "I've been playing against a computer, although I have missed the theological discussions. What about that history buff you fellows have in custody?"

"Had, old bean, HAD. We released him twenty minutes ago. Lack of evidence, you know . . . or at least that's what he thinks."

"Then you've got him under surveillance."

"Certainly. Given enough rope he'll hang himself. And I'm very much interested in any confederates that might be skulking about. He's a common sailor—not the smartest chap I've ever met."

"Off what ship?" I inquired.

Twigg took a notebook from his pocket, flipped it open without breaking stride, and ran a finger down the page.

"The King Richard—birthed in the London Docks, pier seventeen. The man's name is Samuel Drummond. He was vague about almost everything else."

"Including," Weston probed, "those paintings he was so bent on admiring?"

"Oh, those! The only one he could identify was a macabre concoction called 'At the Point of a Knife.' I'll show it to you before you leave."

"Please do." Geoff glanced through one of the arches that lined the corridor. "For now I'd be content just to know the rationale of this place."

"You would?"

Twigg stopped and pointed helpfully into the chamber.

"It's really quite simple. Those flowers painted on the walls are for atmosphere. The stone cottage in the corner was excavated by archaeologists and rebuilt. And the display cases are chocked full of charred relics. This is the room portraying the great London fire. Each exhibit is devoted to some different aspect of British history. If you take the tour route rather than cutting through the centre as we're now doing, everything's pretty much in chronological order."

"My hat would be off to you," Weston kidded, "if I wore one. What delivery and poise! When you're too old to chase down villains, you can always have a job guiding tourists through—"

"You're impossible," the Inspector concluded with a grin. "Fortunately the Victoria Room is only a little farther on. After you snoop around there a while, perhaps you can prevail on the curator to show you the rest of the place—that is, if you can tear him away from bothering my men. He's rather like a mother hen protecting her chicks."

"How long has he been here?"

"All day, as nearly as I can tell. He was in the storeroom assembling a new display when the crime took place. I think you all will get along famously. He's an odd bird. A little balmy, if you ask me."

"I didn't," Weston assured him.

We walked on in a silence broken only by the clinking of our heels on stone. The hallway was nearly a city block long and seemed unending. Savage Saxon warriors glared at us from the left, to be replaced by the innards of a medieval castle on our right. The signing of the Magna Carta in a field yielded to the terror of the blitz. Stonehenge followed Tyndale's Bible to be succeeded in turn by Henry the Eighth, the sinking of the Spanish Armada, and the marvelous Spinning Jenny. Brushed aluminum showcases, blank-eyed dummies, machinery, tools, fossils and paintings assaulted our senses at too rapid a pace for us to really take them in. It crossed my mind that perhaps this *was* a symbolic crypt—the collected works of a million dead men and women. I wondered how many besides Tyndale were in heaven . . . and how many were screaming in hell.

"The Queen Victoria room's next on your left," Twigg announced at length. "You'll notice the smoky odor." He glanced disapprovingly at Geoff's shirt. "But then you shouldn't mind. I see you're dressed for a luau."

Weston didn't respond. He seemed caught up in the spirit of the place.

We followed the Inspector through the next arch and encountered a dismal sight. The queen to our left was reduced to a heap of wax, plastic, scorched cloth and rubble. And her attendants were also badly damaged. Two had melted faces. And Prince Albert's regal arm was drooping. Buckingham Palace looked ready for a fire sale. Display cases in the center of the room were strewn with shattered glass. Disraeli's and Gladstone's portraits on the rear wall were crooked. The London to Balmoral telegraph had seen better days. And a model of an ocean-going steamship along the right wall had its stacks pried loose. What the thief hadn't defaced the Yard had left askew in its search for the booty. Only the Victoria Cross hung stately and undisturbed in a small show window built into the left side of the arch.

A low whistle escaped my lips.

"I say, no wonder the curator is in a tizzy! This place looks like it's been visited by a wrecking crew."

"The value of the diamonds," Twigg glowered, "is slightly over three million pounds. And minor disorder is a small price to pay for their recovery."

"If," Geoffrey ammended, "they're hidden here at all. Please be good enough to fetch the gentleman in charge of the collections. While you're gone, John and I will have a look around."

"I'm sure you will." The Inspector buttoned up his coat in preparation for more cultured company. "My men should still be working in this part of the building, so I won't be long. Be careful not to get glass in your knees when you go crawling around." He turned and strode toward the archway.

Geoffrey couldn't resist chuckling.

"If we do," he shot after our guide, "we'll try not to bleed on the evidence."

As the Inspector disappeared around the corner, Weston stuck his hands on his hips and surveyed the wreckage.

"John, you start over there at the smashed case. Don't bother to check for fingerprints. I imagine the Yard already has three or four hundred partials. And we can hardly hope to compete with them in matters of routine. Check for any little thing out of the ordinary. I think I'll have a look at the late, lamented queen. She may have been burned as a diversion to buy the thief some time, but there is another possibility."

I opened the valise and extracted tweezers and a magnifier for Geoffrey as well as a lens and wisk broom for myself. Now fully armed, we set to work. True to form I began on all fours—sweeping a clear path to the case. It wouldn't do to smash a clue unthinkingly. And the marble floor was so flecked with colors that it was next to impossible to make out small objects. All I discovered, however, was a bountiful supply of dirt and glass slivers. My partner didn't seem to be faring much better. Whenever I looked over he had his nose to the lens and was methodically picking through ashes. But his evidence envelopes remained in his pocket—still unused.

After clearing a path around the display table, I scrambled to my feet and trained my magnifier on its contents—or lack of them. Each empty space was neatly labeled in gothic print. There was only one exception. The Duchess of York's necklace for some peculiar reason remained untouched. A four- or five-carat diamond along with several smaller stones twinkled at me from massive gold settings. Out of curiosity I slid on a glove and hefted it. The Duchess must have been a regular Amazon! The bauble weighed a good three pounds.

"Have a look here." I held the thing up for Geoffrey's benefit. "It's no wonder jewelry like this went out of style. My neck aches in empathy just to think of someone wearing it."

Geoffrey looked my way only after coaxing a fragment into his pouch. But when he saw what I had, his voice betrayed excitement.

"Bring it on over, old bean. I think you've latched onto something."

"With pleasure." I made my way along the swept path and ambled across to the dummies. "There doesn't seem to be any marks around the settings," I volunteered. "Our thief just doesn't appear to like the gaudy."

"I suppose." Weston took the necklace from my hand and held it under his lens. He peered closely along its entire length. "No," he agreed reluctantly, "there hasn't been any attempt to pry gems loose or to cut through the linkage points. Perhaps time was too short . . . although wire cutters would do the job in an instant." He compressed the trinket in his fist until it formed a heap slightly larger than a tennis ball. "For some reason—either size, design, or weight—this piece of jewelry was unstealable. And we've got to find out why. I'm convinced that's the key to finding the rest of the treasure. And speaking of keys . . . have a look at this." He handed me one of the clue envelopes.

I opened the flap and discovered a charred plastic disc.

"You'll notice," my partner helped out, "that nub on one side. As nearly as I can tell it's the width one would expect for the neck of a door key."

"Then the thief must have hidden—"

"In an unused room or broom closet while the guards made their rounds at closing time. Or," Weston ammended, "someone wants us to think that."

"Then you suspect a plant."

My partner considered for a moment.

"Not in the usual sense. The key was at the bottom of the ashes and the ashes were undisturbed. But our rogue could have tossed it at the manikin's feet hoping that guards would quickly extinguish the blaze. I admit, though, the scenario is unlikely. Even sealing the plastic in a water-filled bag wouldn't insure its preservation." He looked over toward the entranceway. "Well, well, the pitter patter of not so little feet! It sounds as though Twigg's returning."

Footsteps could indeed be heard coming down the hall.

"Let's meet them in the corridor," I suggested. "If the guards were on their toes, we may be able to eliminate a few suspects from the running."

"If you mean what I think," Weston smiled in anticipation, "you're not above an occasional play on words yourself."

We followed the clicking sound to the arch and nearly collided with the Inspector as he turned the corner. Twigg stopped just in time and shook his head in disgust.

"You chaps have all the finesse of a herd of bison. Well, here's your curator." He glanced at the bifocaled gentleman behind him. "Sir Thomas Dodd, may I present Mr. John Taylor, Esq.," he indicated me, "and Mr. Geoffrey Weston. Their methods are a trifle unorthodox, but I think you'll find them interesting and thoroughly competent."

Geoff appraised the newcomer—a short, middle-aged chap with a receding hairline.

"It's good to meet you, Sir Thomas. I trust it won't be a bother to answer a few questions. We'll try to make them as brief as possible."

The curator extended a well-manicured hand and smiled disarmingly.

"Not in the least, Mr. Weston." His voice was deep and confident. "After trying to fend off maniacs for the last two hours, I assure you any change is for the better. Have you any idea as yet where the Weatherford collection has gotten off to?"

"None whatsoever," my partner admitted. "But there are several intriguing possibilities. I assume that the guards have been cleared of any complicity."

Sir Thomas brushed some lint off his jacket sleeve.

"Dear me, I should hope so. Your Inspector," he said, glancing disdainfully at Twigg, "has been *inspecting* them ever since he arrived. The poor creatures have been drugged, polygraphed, mesmerized and, for all I know, sanforized."

"They have," Twigg interrupted hastily, "voluntarily agreed to certain tests."

"After," the curator concluded with barely concealed anger, "you threatened to interrogate them until dawn if they didn't. This is not a police state, Inspector, and you had better jolly well realize that fact."

Twigg shifted uneasily—well aware of Sir Thomas' political clout.

"Weston," he advised with all the official dignity he could muster, "the guards seem to be in the clear. That leaves us with only Sam Drummond as a suspect. He had motive. Sailors aren't all that well paid. He had opportunity. And he refused to take the polygraph test."

"And what," I asked, "did the soles of his shoes look like?"

The Inspector looked at me as though I'd taken leave of my senses.

"How should I know? I'm no cobbler! Most probably they were rough and sort of rounded on—"

"Were there," I insisted, "any glass fragments imbedded in the leather? The thief had to walk over glass, you know, after he smashed the case."

Twigg looked positively ill. His face reddened a shade or two and he appeared tempted to bang it against a wall.

"We . . . For all I knew the guards had already brought him into the Victoria Room and . . ."

"In other words," my partner ventured sympathetically, "you confronted him with the empty case in your attempt to obtain a confession."

The Inspector swallowed hard. "Unfortunately, that's about what happened."

"Don't feel too badly about it," Geoff cautioned. "We'll still get our man." He shifted his gaze. "What about you, Sir Thomas? Are your shoes clean?"

The curator smiled broadly. "It's about time, Mr. Weston, that someone has had enough imagination to suspect me. And I'm afraid I'll have to fan the flames of suspicion." He peeked over his glasses like the little old watchmaker and lowered his voice to a stage whisper. "I was called in to catalogue the losses. Unfortunately my feet are as glass-studded as the thief's or the Inspector's."

Geoffrey studied the man's expression with a measure of respect. "I admire your attitude," he concluded. "But you are, you know, the most likely candidate for prosecution—assuming, of course, that the jewels are not found in this building. I advise you to be careful in what you say."

Dodd's smile wavered ever so slightly. But he managed to keep it glued in place. His voice remained firm also, but not nearly so friendly.

"Would you please explain that statement."

"Certainly." Geoffrey weighed his next words carefully. "Do you as curator have master keys to every lock in the annex?"

"Of course I do. Go on."

"And does that include the outer doors?"

"It does."

Weston held the necklace up to the light and turned it over absentmindedly in his fingers as he considered.

"Then, Sir Thomas, you could have spirited the jewels outside in either of two ways. The first possibility is, I admit, rather uninspired. Let's assume that the outer doors operate at differing speeds. You've noticed the inconsistency. So you wait until the guards pass by and then unlock the fastest door. At the proper moment you smash the case, light the fire, and depend on the smoke alarm to open your entrance just enough so you can toss the booty through to a friend. I'm sure Inspector Twigg will check out the electric motors to see if a hairline crack at the main entrance means a wider opening anywhere else."

"Your idea seems rather farfetched," Dodd objected. "How could I know that everyone would leave the front controls? If the override had been pushed sooner, the doors might not have budged."

"That, of course, is the weakness of the theory." Geoffrey turned the matter in his mind. "But even if your chances were only fifty-fifty, it might have been worth a try. You could always drop the jewels and walk away undetected. I personally prefer the second possibility, however. It explains a few more of the facts."

"Come now," Twigg interrupted testily. "You're harassing this gentleman. Wild theories aren't going to—"

"Shut up, Twigg," Sir Thomas demanded. "You've been both inept and boorish in conducting this investigation. And I resent having you as a defender. Mr. Weston, proceed with your accusation—if that's what it is."

Geoff smiled in spite of himself. The man was indeed a character.

"Thank you. Let's start with an assumption. The bulk of the stolen gems were unmounted, were they not?"

"All but two brooches."

"Then it would have been a fairly simple matter to forge copies of them."

Dodd frowned and looked past us into the Victoria Room. His voice was contemplative—almost detached.

"Yes, I suppose it would."

"I see you already have an idea where I'm going." Weston eyed the suspect keenly. "You possess keys to the display tables. You might, therefore, have replaced the real jewels with fakes, carried the diamonds home a few at a time, and then staged this robbery."

"But," I protested, "that still wouldn't explain the disappearance of the forgeries. We're right back where we started."

"Not quite," Sir Thomas disagreed. "Your partner is well aware that a fire can serve a double purpose. I assume you're suggesting, Weston, that the forgeries were flammable."

"It had," Geoff admitted, "crossed my mind. What do you think the chances are that you burned the contents of the showcase at the Queen's feet?"

Thomas Dodd scrutinized each one of us in turn.

"I think," he concluded soberly, "that I need an advocate." His hands shook ever so slightly as he pulled a wallet out of his hip pocket and fumbled through it. Finally finding a business card, he handed it to Geoff. "I am indebted to you, sir, for giving such a candid analysis. It's wrong, I assure you, but now I know where I stand. If you devise any other ways that diamonds can be smuggled off the premises, would you please give me a call?"

Geoff shook his head firmly in the negative.

"I'm afraid that is out of the question. My first consideration has to be the best interests of my client. But rest assured we will try to determine *every* method by which the crime could have been committed."

"Then that will have to do."

"Indeed it will."

Almost without looking Geoff tossed the necklace to Twigg—whose reflexes proved excellent.

"Inspector, if I put that trinket in my evidence bag, some eyebrows will raise. Would you please place it under lock and key. I also will require blueprints of this building. Have them sent to Baker Street this evening if possible. And, oh yes, you might start visiting local fences to discourage them from making purchases."

"I'll get right to it." Twigg's tone was clipped and businesslike. "And those door motors will be examined. Do you have anything to ask the guards?"

"That can be postponed until after church to-morrow. Meanwhile, you might have an expert check the computer system for tampering. I don't believe we'll be needing you anymore here. Sir Thomas can give us the guided tour."

Our friend plopped the last of the Weatherford collection into a brown envelope and sealed and initialed the flap. His expression was sombre.

"I was about to make a similar suggestion," he commented. "You have a way of adding to a body's workload. In addition to your errands, there's still the matter of searching this place." Without waiting for a reply, Twigg turned and strode off down the hall.

"One last thing," Weston called after him. "Keep me posted on that sailor, Sam Drummond."

*   *   *   *   *

We now began a room-by-room trek through history. But it was a different kind of tour—including such points of interest as air-conditioning ducts, closets, lighting panels, and storerooms. On occasion we nodded to bobbies at work or detoured around the results of their labors. Wall gratings lay scattered on the floor. Electrical outlets dangled from wiring. Sink traps in every bathroom had been dismantled. Acoustical paneling was ripped from the ceiling. After over an hour's walking we dragged ourselves into the first of the twentieth-century chambers. Thomas Dodd looked down forlornly at a radar set whose innards now spewed forth in disarray.

"Those men," he choked, "are heartless."

I gave him an understanding pat on the back.

"They're only doing their job," I reminded him. "And a cleanup team will repair most of the damage."

"What's more," Geoffrey encouraged, "they'll find the jewels for you if the things are still here . . . assuming for the sake of argument you're not guilty. There's only one hiding place that has a chance at escaping the Yard's notice."

"What's that?"

"A pre-fabricated showcase." My partner smiled. "Put the diamonds on display and they become invisible. Anywhere less obvious, 'by the book' procedures will unearth them without fail. You might browse around checking collections after we leave."

"I'll do that." In spite of the air conditioning the curator mopped his brow. "It's torture to just stand around feeling helpless."

Geoffrey nodded his head in agreement. His voice softened.

"I know what you mean. If you don't turn up anything, try looking through the Tyndale Room."

"You think the answer to the mystery might be there?"

"I believe," my partner replied warmly, "that the answer to the biggest mystery of all is there. We'll talk about it later. For now would you point us in the direction of a certain painting. I believe it's called 'The Knife Point' or something of the sort. We'll find it ourselves."

Dodd's face brightened.

"That would be 'At the Point of a Knife' by Franz König. As a matter of fact, it's in the next chamber. Just walk on through that arch and you

can't miss it." He indicated the second of the twentieth-century rooms.

Sir Thomas turned out to be a prophet. We
couldn't miss it. When Geoff and I entered and
scanned the walls, one single painting on the right
riveted our attention. As we walked closer I talked
to myself in a stunned whisper, "No wonder the
sailor remembered it."

On the canvas in front of us a pretty young
lady lay sleeping on an operating table. Her soft,
secret smile spoke of sweet dreams and hopes for a
rosy future. Masked doctors gathered around
studying her with clinical detachment. Chrome
gleamed, machinery hummed, and an expression-
less, anonymous surgeon began sinking a needle
into the girl's abdomen. She didn't seem to mind.
And he was so calm and expert. But inside her
translucent belly a tiny baby cringed and tried to
ward off the spear. Terror and pleading mingled in
its wide eyes as it held out a hand to us. It's silent
scream went unheard. And the "mother" dreamed
on with her Mona Lisa smile.

We stood speechless and caught up in the dra-
ma for several moments. But then Geoffrey
abruptly turned away.

"Come on, John, let's head for Baker Street
where we can be alone. I don't feel very kindly toward the human race right now."

I thought I saw a tear trickle down his cheek.
But then I might have been mistaken. My own
eyes were brimming.

# CHAPTER 3

## *Ersatz Wisdom*

I pushed the button on the stereo and deflated into my easy chair. The tone arm drifted down onto the record. And after a few preliminary crackles, music swelled, flowed and filled the room. But somehow the London Symphony didn't sound the same at midnight as it would have several hours earlier. I formed a mental picture of June Albey and sighed. I missed her openness, animated conversation and—yes—even her American accent. Wellington's Victory on the turntable was a poor substitute for her company.

"You'll have another date next week," Geoff encouraged—fracturing my daydream. "And by that time you may have an adventure or two to share with her."

"I suppose so. I . . . Oh, bother, you've done it again! How did you guess my thoughts this time?"

Weston laid aside his book, leaned back in his chair and smiled.

"John, you do not sigh and stare into space every time Josef Krips raises his baton. It was all too obvious that rosy cheeks, brown eyes and long brown tresses had you snared."

"As bad as that?"

"It was. And I envy you. As a Christian she's tops—never learned to be bored, narrow, or luke-warm. Don't let her get away."

"I'll do my best," I agreed ruefully. "But our clients seem bent on doing the letting. This is the second cancelled date we've had this month. I'm starting a rare collection of unused tickets."

"Every profession," Geoffrey philosophized, "has its drawbacks. But ours has so many pluses, don't you think? Every day is different . . . no nine-to-five humdrum. And we're doing what God equipped us for. We stand for righteousness, root out evil, and clear the innocent. I find the whole process highly satisfying in spite of the danger."

"Speaking of 'clearing the innocent,'" I changed the subject, "what's your impression of Sir Thomas? I find myself liking him and hoping he's not the thief."

Geoff snagged a bottle of peanuts from off the carpet and unscrewed the lid.

"I have to agree with you," he considered. "But I don't think we've much to worry about. There's not one chance in ten thousand that he's guilty."

My mouth dropped open in astonishment.

"But then why did you—"

"I had to, old fellow. I'm almost certain that sailor Drummond is the rogue, but I haven't the foggiest idea how he disposed of the jewels. And with Twigg convinced they were still inside, nothing was being done to prevent an accomplice from fencing them. I had to invent some plausible theory to force the Yard into action before it was too late. Thomas Dodd just happened to be the only chap who fit my story."

"But," I pondered, "if he fits, how do you know you haven't stumbled on the real solution?"

Geoff tossed some peanuts in his mouth and began chewing.

"I don't *know* anything. But I can't quite make myself believe that that burned plastic key was meant to be found. And if it wasn't, then Dodd has to be innocent. He already had metal keys. Why would he need a plastic duplicate? If, on the other hand, someone wanted to cover up tracks and throw suspicion on employees, a flammable master key would be just the—excuse the expression—ticket. And a limey with waterfront connections should not have too much difficulty in procuring one."

"You don't believe Drummond acted alone then?"

"I hope he did. That would simplify matters a good deal. Since he's under surveillance he'd have a real battle selling or recutting the diamonds. But my instincts tell me he had help. Judging from what we've seen so far, he's not the kind of man who would make things easy on us. What's more he . . ."

The clang of the doorbell sliced through the music. I started to my feet but Weston beat me to it and hurried to answer. The bell sounded again as an impatient finger at the gate did calisthenics.

"That's got to be one of Twigg's associates," I commented. "I recognize the touch."

It was. My partner returned from the front yard a moment later carrying a well-stuffed folder. And he was clearly pleased as punch. There was bounce to his step and a twinkle in his eye. He casually slid the package onto the coffee table.

"Things are looking better all the time," he beamed. "A fence has just been arrested with five of the smaller stones. The man claims that's all he bought."

"Could he describe the seller?"

"Of course," Geoff declared tongue-in-cheek. "It was a hunched-backed fellow with a long beard and a mustache."

"In other words," I concluded, "we're now after somebody who deals in disguises."

My partner began spreading papers on the table.

"That's about the size of it. But it's some help to know that much. A black uniform, for example, might facilitate the bloke's approach to the annex. Now let me see. . . . What do we have here?" Geoff picked up several sheets of blueprints and rapidly sifted through them—stopping to study the wiring diagram to the security system.

I walked around behind him and stooped to have a look over his shoulder. It was clear why Geoff had paused.

"What a ruddy complicated design!" I shook my head in disbelief. "They must have spent a fortune to install that much spaghetti."

"Security," my partner concurred with a sigh, "is seldom cheap. And even then it's never sure. There are five back-up circuits here, but the gems are gone. You know, old bean, I'm glad we're not rich. I much prefer storing up treasures in heaven where they won't be burgled."

"And," I added, "having peace of mind down here. But, I must say, I won't reject a reward if we stumble on the diamonds. Those independent missionaries we met in Tibet looked like they could use a bit more meat in their diet."

Weston fixed his gaze on the next sheet.

"Indeed they did. Money can prove very beneficial if it's not hoarded. Well, well, look at this. Twigg must have had a department artist draw us a simplified floor plan. Very considerate of him since the architect's sketches leave out room names. And here's something interesting. You'll notice that that oil painting we saw is almost on a direct line between the Victoria Room and the left side door. What's more, the left and rear entrances are both relatively close to the crime scene."

"Of course! Then you think Drummond remembers 'At the Point of a Knife' because he passed it while getting rid of the diamonds."

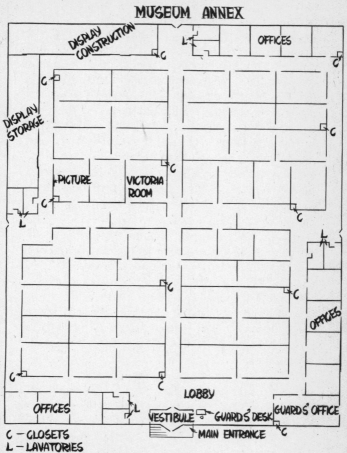

# MUSEUM ANNEX

DISPLAY CONSTRUCTION

OFFICES

C

L

C

DISPLAY STORAGE

C

C

PICTURE

VICTORIA ROOM

C

C

L

C

C

C

OFFICES

C

OFFICES

C

LOBBY

OFFICES

L

VESTIBULE

GUARD'S DESK

GUARD'S OFFICE

MAIN ENTRANCE

C

C — CLOSETS
L — LAVATORIES

"Or," my colleague ammended, "while returning from the task. Of course, it's always possible
that he toured the museum first to soak up information in support of his alibi. But, if so, you'd
think he would remember more than one painting.
John, I should be the next couple of hours going
over the building plans, and I see the Inspector's
also included some biographical material on Dodd
and the guards. While I'm doing my homework,
would you examine the evidence that's over there
on the workbench. The key is obviously of private
manufacture, so you won't learn much from it.
But the fragments in the other envelope are from a
petrol-filled bottle. See if you can find out what it
contained before being converted into a molotov
cocktail."

"Why not?" I forced a smile. "After all, we've
got nearly six hours until dawn and there aren't
over a hundred thirty thousand kinds of bottles in
this city."

Geoffrey stifled a yawn.

"As I said, every profession has its drawbacks.
You'd best get started while you're still fresh." He
looked down at the papers and didn't speak another word.

As the wall clock ticked monotonously on, I
made a spectroscopic analysis of the fragments
and then began paging through looseleaf cata-
logues in search of a matching sample. Over the
years we've built up quite a collection of glass,
paper, cloth, and other odds and ends likely to be
of use to us. In this instance the collection proved

adequate. The broken pieces were from a bottle of Wild Boar ale. After making that discovery at a little past three in the morning, I trudged wearily off to bed. Weston was still valiantly engaged in "homework," but I noticed he was beginning to nod.

* * * * *

The sermon the next morning was about Achan—who stole forbidden gold and silver and hid them under his tent. Joshua then followed the Lord's instructions and unmasked the thief by casting lots. As I listened, I was impressed anew by God's holy zeal. I'll admit I also envied Joshua's supernatural guidance. Dice like those would come in very handy in the Weatherford diamond case. For the seventh or eighth time since beginning the investigation I had a heart-to-heart talk with the Lord about that insurance man Wiggens and the British Museum. Judging from Geoff's long silences, he was also sensing the need to pray.

When we arrived home from the early service, my partner retired to the bedroom to change into something more comfortable while I popped muffins in the toaster and poured the juice. The aroma of hot bread and raisins had just begun to tantalize my nostrils when the jangle of the telephone interrupted the quiet.

"I'll get it!"

I set the jug of apple juice down on the kitchen table, covered the glasses to keep the flies away, and stepped into the living room.

"Hallo."

Inspector Twigg's voice sounded metallic in my ear.

"Hallo. Is that you, John?"

"Of course it is, Inspector. To what do I owe the pleasure?"

"To your partner's pushiness. I've got that update he asked for on Drummond. You'll never believe where he is right now!"

I glanced at my watch.

"Since it's eleven thirty-five, Sunday morning, I believe I can take a wild stab."

"And you'd be right," Twigg conceded. "But I didn't think sailors were that religious anymore. Then again, this chap certainly needs help. It seems he just got back from a salvage expedition in which sharks ate his diving partner. So he visits a museum to take his mind off his troubles and ends up practically accused of the decade's largest jewel robbery. How's that for being jinxed!"

"I wouldn't know," I observed. "I don't believe in jinxes. Where did the fellow spend the night?"

"On board ship. In fact, he went there directly from the museum. That would make things look a little black for Sir Thomas, wouldn't you say?"

"You're right," I yawned. "I wouldn't say. Where is Drummond sitting right now?"

"Hold on a second." Paper shuffled in the background. "He's on the last pew . . . at the extreme right side of the church near the door. Doesn't appear he likes to socialize at the end of services. Not that he could do much of that anyway. There aren't over thirty or forty people in the whole sanctuary. I suppose you're thinking of going over to ask him a few questions."

"If we can get there on time. Where is it?"

"Down on the waterfront. The name's St. Albans. Let me dig up the address." More papers rattled followed by a loud clunk as he dropped the receiver and another as he retrieved it. "You still there?"

"Yes. Go on."

"Well," Twigg chuckled, "here's a bit of irony. It's only about five blocks south of Lloyds—on Lower Thames Street across from the Billingsgate Market. I hope you don't mind the smell of fish."

"Not if it's fresh," I assured him. "Thanks for the information."

"Don't mention it. The Yard pays the phone bill. Ta ta."

I returned to the kitchen deep in thought. That shark attack added an ominous hue to the case that hadn't been there before. Geoffrey was still dressing, so I thanked the Lord for the muffin and proceeded to demolish it. When my colleague ambled into the room I filled him in on the Inspector's revelations. As Weston listened, his jaw set.

"I don't like the sound of this at all," he declared at last. "Salvage operations mean money. Divers have the closest look at what's on the bottom. One diver is dead and another is probably a thief. What does that suggest to you?"

"When you put it that way," I frowned, "*murder*. Here's hoping you're wrong."

Geoffrey gulped down the juice and added his glass to the pile in the sink.

"Put out some food for Gladstone," he ordered, "while I clear the table. It's time we had a talk with Mr. Drummond. If we miss him, I'll settle for a chat with his pastor. I want to know that sailor inside and out!"

There was very little traffic at that time of day, and we were able to strike a rapid pace. The engine of the Mercedes droned with steady power as we turned up Oxford and continued on it through several name changes. Oxford is one of those odd streets built over the centuries as separate roads but now connected to traverse the city. Soon we were passing a couple blocks south of the museum on New Oxford. Then the street name was Holborn and we sped just north of the Patent Office's high gabled windows. The Holborn circus connected to Holborn Viaduct which was renamed Newgate Street as we passed the stark, domed Central Criminal Courts building. When the road, now Cheapside Poultry, reached the Bank of England, we left it and headed south toward the river. Geoff was driving. I was familiarizing myself with the museum plans.

"The annex," I concluded at last, "doesn't appear to me to have any design flaws. Were *you* able to detect any?"

"None." Weston's voice was grim. "But one mustn't overlook the possibility that the plans are in error."

"Jolly good," I brightened. "Then you suspect

the builders put in some secret passageway."

Geoffrey slowed and steered right on to King William Street.

"I doubt that," he considered. "On a project this size, hundreds of workers would have to know about it. I doubt if anyone could bribe them all to silence. It is possible, though, that some small structural change was made through carelessness or shortage of materials. We'll have to take a peek around the grounds when we get a chance. Perhaps the outside of the building will tell us more than its interior did."

"What," I asked in exasperation, "about the dossiers on the personnel? I haven't had time to go through them."

"I'm afraid they're just as unsatisfying as the building plans—full of facts but saying nothing. Dodd comes up clean as a whistle, of course. He's not extremely rich—who is nowadays—but he's well fixed. And the guards are all respected, middle-class family men. After reading their profiles I don't even feel like chatting with them. Cyril Holcomb is the only one with substantial debts, and he's managing to make regular payments. Well, here we are."

Our station wagon turned the corner and decelerated as we encountered women and children crossing the street to market. Pungent smells permeated the air, mingling with the shrill voices of vendors and buyers.

"Now there," Weston pointed out his window, "is a church that could really have a leaflet ministry. All the members have to do is walk a few yards."

"Or," I added, "sail paper airplanes from the front steps. But I have a feeling they're not all that active. The place looks awfully run-down."

It did for a fact. The red brick walls were solid enough, but coated with grime. No bell hung in the tower. And the stained-glass windows were pocked with holes—some covered with cardboard. Neighborhood toughs had thrown their stones until the rector had evidently given up making repairs as a bad show. This was a typical inner city church—too old to be really respectable, but too new to be appreciated as an antique. The only untypical thing about it was a neatly manicured lawn on one side in front of the rectory.

I got out of the Mercedes, slammed the door and joined Weston on the sidewalk.

"We may be a trifle late," I observed with disappointment. "There doesn't seem to be any singing or preaching."

"You may be right." Geoff ran a comb through his hair and tucked in his shirt. "But it's only five after twelve. Somebody should still be around."

The two of us strode side by side up the walk and climbed the steps. But when I tried the knob the thick oaken doors wouldn't budge.

"This is a fine kettle of fish," I complained. "Churches are supposed to be launching pads, not fortresses!"

"It's a sign of the times, John. Let's look for a

side entrance. If that fails we can always try the rectory."

For some reason churches almost never have signs directing one to the pastor's office. And St. Albans was no different. We tried three doors without success before finally finding our way into the basement. It was a damp place—no doubt from its closeness to the waterfront. And my nose itched from the dust. I had the feeling of being in a dungeon, except that each chamber along the hall was equipped with Lilliputian chairs, slateboards, and moldy picture books. There wasn't a leg iron in sight. Neither was there any evidence of use. Perhaps ours were the only footprints that had echoed down the corridor in the last ten years.

We discovered a circular staircase up front and trusted our weight to its creaking boards. It wound around twice and came out at length in a barren vestibule. The only sound that met my ears was the methodical dripping of a water pipe somewhere. I tapped my partner on the shoulder and ventured a whisper.

"This place gives me goose bumps. Perhaps Twigg sent us to the wrong church."

"Hardly likely," Geoff assured me in a hushed tone. "Nearly eight hundred were declared 'surplus' last year, but this one's still a hop and a jump away from that. Notice the floor's been swept on this level. I think they held services."

I followed Weston into the sanctuary—treading softly as old lumber gave slightly under my feet. Unlit lanterns hung suspended from rafters, and colored sunlight trickled through narrow windows. I had an impression of spaciousness and gloom. Geoff, now all business, walked over to the last row of pews.

"John, while we're here let's have a look at the underside of these benches. There's just a chance . . . but surely the Inspector's man would have caught it if that had happened. Have you got your mini-torch with you?"

In answer I took it out and worked the switch. A narrow beam of light illumined well-worn mahogany.

"The back row," I agreed, "would be an ideal place for a drop. Nobody would be behind to see you pull a package from under the next seat."

"Or," Geoffrey added, "to witness anyone handing you a stack of money in a Book of Common Prayer."

I slid under the next to last row of pews and began my inspection. The underside looked practically new—protected by three generations of chewing gum. It didn't take long, however, to detect a change in tradition. Near the far end a piece of masking tape was dangling between blobs of gum.

"Give me some tweezers," I demanded in triumph. "It looks as though Drummond has gotten his payoff. And we might just find a fingerprint."

My partner handed them to me and I gently peeled the tape from the wood. In a moment I'd clambered out and set up shop for processing prints. The pew became my workbench.

"Go light with your powder on the sticky side," Weston cautioned. "You might just get a negative print of whoever taped the package there."

I tried. But if there had been any whirls, contact with the wood had mashed them to nothingness. The back of the tape, however, was a different story. As I brushed away the dark powder we use on light surfaces, one clear fingerprint and a partial came into view. I fixed them on with celophane tape and then sealed up the evidence in an envelope. After scribbling both the date, location and my initials on the flap, I passed it to Geoff who countersigned before stuffing it in his pocket. I snapped my kit closed and stood up straight.

"I presume now we have a little talk with the pastor about who sat in front of Drummond."

"We do, indeed," Weston concurred. He looked around hopefully for a new direction in which to search. "Let's try that door by the right-hand pulpit. It would make sense for an office to be on the side closest the rectory."

"Provided," I added, "it's not *in* the rectory."

Geoffrey took the lead as we hurried up the aisle. The door opened inward to reveal yet another door a few steps beyond with a ribbon of light shining from beneath it. My partner strode forward and knocked. There was a sound of movement on the other side—then a booming, resonant greeting.

"I say, who can that be. Come in. Come in!"

Geoff twisted the knob and we entered the study. Drab unpainted walls and spartan furnishing seemed out of place as we confronted the gentleman. He was every inch the extrovert—bouncing out of his chair and leaning over the desk to extend chubby fingers.

"Good to see you, chaps. Good to see you. Oh, excuse me!" He paused to wipe shoe polish off his hand before reoffering it to us. "Only have one pair of shoes, you see, and I've just been shining them. Now, what may I do for you?"

My partner shook his hand heartily.

"You may, sir, help us solve a most baffling mystery. I'm Geoffrey Weston and this is my partner, John Taylor, Esq. May I present my card."

The cleric took and studied it with a look of surprise:

Sleuths, Ltd.
London's Consulting Detective Firm
Number 31, Baker Street

"Why, this is incredible," he chortled. "Me visited by the great Geoffrey Weston. I read about you only last week in the *Telegraph*. Please be seated. Pull up a chair. Have a smoke." He held out a box.

"We don't," I responded. "Thanks anyway. Bad for the lungs and heart, you know." Geoff and I eased into identical straight-backed chairs.

"Of course," our host agreed. "A nasty habit. I've been trying to break it for years. Andrew Cook at your service. What's your problem?" He folded his hands and looked at us in rosy-cheeked expectation—oblivious to the perspiration trickling down his clerical collar.

"We have reason to believe," my colleague began, "that one of your parishioners has been involved in a crime. And we'd appreciate any information you could give us about him."

"Oh, dear me! Not another one!" Pastor Cook rubbed his eye nervously. "Which one of the young Turks is it this time? We have a lot of seamen stop by off and on, you know."

"A fellow by the name of Sam Drummond. I believe he was in church this morning seated on the back row."

Rev. Cook stared past us as though trying to picture the young man mentally.

"Drummond . . . Drummond. Oh, you mean the big-shouldered chap with a scar on his lip. Curses a lot, he does. I once went swimming with him. That's why he comes to mind. As I said, those sailors are always in and out—never stay long or come regular. I believe he *was* here today, though."

"Would you," Weston prodded, "tell us everything you know about him."

"Of course. But I'm afraid that's not much. He joked a lot but never really talked about himself. Never had any friends to speak of. I'm afraid I was just a casual acquaintance myself. What did he do?"

My colleague brushed aside the question.

"Did Drummond come alone today?"

"He was always alone," Cook replied. "Even in a crowd."

"And who was sitting in the pew directly in front of him?"

The rector picked up a pencil and began chewing on its end. He looked over at the bookcase without really seeing it.

"I'm sorry I can't help you there, Mr. Weston. It could have been another sailor. But then I seem to remember an elderly lady somewhere near the back. I don't normally pay attention to such things. Too busy thinking about the sermon. We had a good one today . . . on the parable of Jonah. You should have been here yourself."

Weston's eyes narrowed.

"Reverend Cook," he shared honestly, "there are many things I admire about you. You have a good personality. You evidently are serving here in spite of a low stipend and a small congregation. But in all honesty you've just told me why your assembly is dying."

A puzzled frown flickered across the rector's face. He cleared his throat before responding.

"Tell me whatever it is you're getting at. I won't deny I'm concerned about reduced attendance, and I'm always open to new ideas."

Before answering, Geoff stood—stretching his frame to its full six foot three inches—and stepped over to the bookcase. He began scanning the shelves.

"I'd say," he suggested, "that that's your problem. You're entirely too open to new ideas. Look at these authors: Heidegger, Bultmann, Tillich. You've collected half the religious radicals of the last century! The book of Jonah isn't a parable, and you're strangling your congregation by teaching that it is. Explain away miracles, sir, and Christianity goes down the drain. Your parishioners realize that, even if you don't."

The rector fought to maintain a dignified front. But he was clearly uncomfortable. His cordial attitude seemed to evaporate into thin air.

"I'll have you know that I have studied at some of the most respected schools in England. I know what's best for my people. And I don't appreciate—"

"I'm sure you don't," Weston cut in. "And I don't appreciate liars."

"What do you mean by that!"

"I mean that you just told me you were *always* open to new ideas, but you seem decidedly closed to what I'm saying."

"I wasn't aware," Cook smiled crookedly, "that your ideas were new. They seemed rather ancient and covered with cobwebs actually. But make your point if you must. Be quick about it."

My partner took a large volume from the bookcase and commenced leafing through it.

"Do you, Cook, consider yourself an existentialist . . . a form critic?"

"I do."

"Why?"

"Why?" The rector seemed taken aback. "Well . . . I suppose because the system permits me to . . . to apply God's Word to my own life here and now. Biblical myths convey truths that are, after all, quite gratifying."

Weston frowned.

"Don't you see, pastor, that you've just made a nonsense statement?" He slammed the book closed. "If the Bible contains *myths* of any kind . . . even if you redefine the word to try to expunge the idea of untruthfulness that clings to it, then the Bible ceases to function. You become a little tin god with a shopping basket—accepting what you want and discarding the rest into some nice-sounding poetic limbo."

"I am merely," Cook disagreed, "rediscovering the methods by which the early church wrote Scripture as they strung liturgical stories together."

"You're good at paraphrasing Bultmann," my partner responded. "But stop and think, man. Think of the implications of what you're saying! Bultmann 'demythologized' away most of the Bible and left only a core that he thought authentic. But once he'd done that he had no objective grounds for defending even the core. So one of his disciples, Fritz Buri, buried the rest! Yours isn't a new idea. It's a dead one!"

Andrew Cook sighed and looked at his watch.

"Really, Mr. Weston, this conversation isn't getting us anywhere. You're brilliant enough in your own field, but, honestly, what sane man could accept an errorless Bible! There are the archaeological problems. And remember that genius Albert Schweitzer's *Quest for the Historical Jesus.*

Why did he conclude that Jesus was a real person rather than an ideal fictional character? Because Jesus made a *mistake* in thinking the kingdom was about to come! I'm afraid you're a Don Quixote tilting at windmills. Leave matters of scholarly interpretation to the scholars."

I could see that Geoff was disturbed by the preacher's smug attitude. But he kept hold of his feelings. His voice, when he spoke, was soft and reasonable.

"Schweitzer, sir, never found the real historical Jesus because he began with the wrong presuppositions. And neither, I'm afraid, have you. You label me insane for believing that God isn't a bumbler. But let me point to a certain archbishop of Canterbury who holds my view. And I could name fifty modern theologians that echo my sentiments. Do you label such men as Packer, Schaeffer, Montgomery (and I could go on and on) as lunatics? Somehow they can read Jesus' statements about the kingdom and see inspiring truth—not error. The King himself was already present. The kingdom in its larger sense could come at *any* instant. Beautiful!"

"Could it?" Cook was critical. "What about the cross? Didn't that have to come first?"

"Of course it did," Weston agreed. "But remember that Jesus predicted as much. He offered the kingdom to Israel but at the same time knew they would reject it. It's interesting, isn't it, that you're arguing from the Bible now as though you really believed it."

"I'm merely accommodating myself," the rector assured him, "to your method of reasoning. Have you finished filling me with your 'new' ideas? If so, I suggest—"

"I have only one further thing to say," Weston interrupted, "and then we'll be leaving. In the nineteenth century, before the bulk of archaeological research, a few chaps noticed that some biblical kings were as yet unknown to science, some words of Scripture similar to expressions used by later cultures. So they cried 'Error, error!' and invented several ignorant authors for each book—authors who supposedly used tag words in their writings. But then, woe is me, they found authors' trademark words spilling over into each other's sections. So what did they do? Junk the system as worthless? Not after all that hard work! They invented more and more new authors to justify their crazy system until every other sentence was believed to be by some new editor. Then people like you jumped in. Still unwilling to abandon the foolishness, they concluded that there were so many writers they could never identify them. What was important was the existential truth and the error-filled form. In the meantime, Cook, archaeologists had discovered the missing kings, verified biblical dates, shown the ancient nature of words, and resolved nearly all the problems that had caused the early scholars to go on their wild goose chase. And where does that leave you? On top of a pyramid built on air! That's where. New discoveries have rendered the new old and the old new. And you need to accept the real historical Jesus as your Savior—the one who paid for your sins on the cross and arose *bodily*."

"That's all very interesting," the rector remarked in a tone that implied it wasn't. "But I assure you I'm quite content with my own inner leap of faith. And I feel you've oversimplified history somewhat. You evangelicals have a knack for that." He rose to his feet. "Now if you'll be so good as to stand by your promise to leave, I'll be able to get to my studies."

Weston pushed himself from his chair and stared with evident disappointment at the pudgy little preacher.

"I hope," he mused, "that you'll think back on what we said at a time when your professionalism isn't threatened. If you ever wish to speak with us, you have our address."

"I'm quite sure I won't use it," Cook declined levelly. "Good day, gentlemen. Have a nice afternoon."

"The same to you." Geoff turned toward me. "Come, John, let's see a boat about a man."

We sauntered across the dingy, carpetless floor and closed the door behind us. A side entrance in the anteroom opened to the outside world, so my partner and I headed that way. Unfastening the latch, we were greeted by bright, clean air and the beautiful sound of hawkers selling fish.

# CHAPTER 4

## *Lumps*

Britannia may no longer ride the waves. But as we approached the London Docks, it was brought home to me again—in cinemascope and Technicolor—that the sea is still England's lifeblood. Thames lighters in great profusion were moored in the artificial lake, awaiting loads of coal or timber for transport upstream. Interspersed with these clumsy, double-nosed craft, river tugs plied their trade. And occasionally a more elegant shallow-draft ship made an appearance. According to the map in my lap, the vessel a quarter mile up the shoreline was one of these. Our Mercedes was drawing near pier seventeen.

Since Geoffrey didn't relish turning the motorcar around on the pier, we stopped just short of it and walked out over the water. The boards under our feet were as thick and solid as railroad ties. The ship in front of us appeared to be a large, con-

verted coast guard cutter of World War II vintage.
It was not so much old as dignified. And someone
had restored her to mint condition. Sky blue paint
replaced the grey. Not a speck of rust was visible.
The only dirt on her was a ring of diesel soot
around the rim of her single stack. Without paus-
ing in the slightest we began walking up the plank
to her deck. I took a deep breath and hailed
whoever might be on board.

"Ahoy! Is anyone there? We're coming
aboard."

A door opened in one of the cabins and a mus-
cular chap in short sleeves and loose-fitting
trousers walked over to the rail. His full red beard
and mustache gave him a fierce appearance. And I
estimated he could take us both on and beat the
stuffing out of us if he wanted. But his reply was
cordial enough.

"Ahoy there, mates! What's your business?"

"Death," Weston shouted back. "We're detectives come to investigate that shark attack."

As we neared the deck our one-man welcoming
committee held out a calloused hand and helped
us aboard.

"Detectives you say. I'd best see some identification." He studied us with shrewd eyes. "I don't
reckon there's much reason fo' Yarders to be 'ere.
After all, it 'appened in Malta."

Geoff held out a card.

"Actually, we're private. And the accident—if
that's what it was—may tie in with an insurance
matter here. I'm Geoffrey Weston." He gestured

in my direction. "This is my partner, John Taylor. You're . . . ?"

"George Stedders." The man's voice was guttural. "My friends call me 'Tiny.' "

"Then Tiny it is," I assured him. I looked aft and saw nothing unusual except for a gantry crane and a few pontoons lashed to the decks. "What kind of crew does it take to run a ship like this?"

He followed my gaze admiringly.

"Two in the engine room, the cap'n, myself . . . I double as first mate and navigator, Wally . . . he's cook, and a couple o' divers."

Geoff raised his eyebrows.

"You double? What does the union say about that?"

"What does the union . . . Oh, that's jolly good!" Tiny convulsed with laughter and slapped Weston on the back so hard he almost fell overboard.

"Where," I complained, "is the joke? Aren't most crews unionized?"

The first mate fought to regain his composure.

"You'll 'ave to excuse me, mate. It's just that . . . hoo . . . hoo . . . It's just that you don't know Cap'n Cosgrove. If one o' us joined, I think 'e'd 'ave us walk the plank. He's a ruddy communist, 'e is. Says unions is a plot to pacify the workers. What 'e really means is 'e don't want to pay union scale."

"Then," my partner wondered, "why do you work for him? Are positions that tight?"

"For a fact, Mr. Weston. And 'e knows 'e 'as

us over a barrel. But you didn't come 'ere to talk about that."

"No," Geoff admitted, "but I find it interesting nonetheless. I assume that neither Drummond nor the captain are on board. Could you show us to the dead man's cabin and tell us what happened to him?"

"Right you are. In fact, everybody's ashore. And I'll be 'appy to show you 'round. Matter o' fact I been wantin' ta talk ta somebody 'bout wa' 'appened. Mighty strange it was."

We started aft—passing portholes as we walked. Deckplates were scalding from the sun. But the water surrounding the vessel shimmered in dazzling coolness.

"It was a cloudy, calm day," our guide continued. "And we 'adn't seen no shark in mor'n a week. Ol' Skinny—that's Skinny O'Brian—even joked 'e was feelin' lonely. Well, mates, 'e went down an' a whole school o' em tore 'im ta bits. Weren't nothin' left. We never even found 'is tanks."

"How long was it," Weston pondered, "between the time he entered the water and the attack?"

"Not mor'n three or four minutes. It's as if they was awaitin' 'im." Tiny opened wide a cabin door and motioned for us to enter. "Watch yer 'ead and yer feet."

We stooped down, stepped over the ledge, and found ourselves in a cramped twelve-by-twelve cubicle. The bed was a slab folded flush against the wall. When down in position it's outer edge hung suspended on chains. A clothes locker, cheap wooden chair, wash basin, and card table completed the decor. Rivets studded the walls and a single porthole provided the only daylight. Weston flipped on the overhead bulb.

"I see you've made a few alterations," he observed. "Enlarged the place a little . . . added plumbing. It's not bad, but I still prefer our flat. Do you mind if we look around?"

" 'elp yerself. But I gotta stay 'ere an' watch."

Geoff opened the locker and began rummaging through the top shelf.

"I wouldn't have it any other way," he assured the mate. "We might need your assistance. Tell me, what were you diving for at Malta? Some sort of treasure?"

Tiny squinted in concern as I swung the bed open and lifted the mattress pad.

"No," he replied at length. "Leastways I don't think so. It was just an old wooden ship. Didn't have nothin' in it. Mighta been worth somethin' if we coulda floated 'er, but she was too brittle. Woulda fallen to pieces if we'd tried to raise 'er."

Weston held up an elaborately dialed watch.

"Why haven't the personal items been bundled by now and sent to relatives?"

The first mate shrugged.

"Don't think 'e 'as any. Anyway, that's the cap'n's job, not mine."

By this time I'd learned that there was nothing either in or under the mattress. The card table was perfectly empty—devoid of anything stuck to its bottom. The chair was ordinary in every way. And the dead man brushed with Pyrodent tooth powder. There didn't even seem to be any dust on the floor. Weston finished with the top shelf and began separating hangers in the under section— working his way through shirt and trouser pockets. His hand stopped in some blue slacks.

"Good grief! What's this?" He pulled out an inch-wide hunk of something covered with lint. Tiny and I bent forward for a better view. Weston took out his pocket knife and shaved off a piece. "Why it looks like wax!" Weston looked to the first mate. "Tiny, do you know of any use a sailor would have for this?"

Stedders pursed his lips under his beard and considered a moment.

"Not in this century," he growled at length. "The stuff used ta be used for waterproofin' matches an' the like. Can't say as it's worth nuthin' now."

"I see." Geoff's face showed puzzlement. He slowly extracted an evidence envelope from his own pocket. "Do you mind," he inquired, "if we take the lump with us?"

Tiny scratched his head.

"I can't see as it would do no harm. Sure. Why not! Let me know if ya find out what 'e did wi' it."

Weston solemnly nodded assent.

"You can rest assured of that." He sealed up his latest find and continued where he'd left off in the locker. "Tell me, Tiny," he remarked casually, "were Skinny and Sam on good terms?"

"Nobody on the King Richard," the mate confided, "is friends wi' Drummond. 'e was born wi' a crab in 'is crib. But Skinny got as close as anyone I guess. Probably the best friend Drummond 'ad. Sam was real quiet after the accident, 'e was."

Geoff stood up straight and slammed the locker closed.

"Well, John, we've done about all we can here. I take it you haven't found any time bombs or shark suits."

"Not so as you'd notice," I smiled. "The place was too shipshape. Where do we go from here?"

"It's a pleasant day," Weston observed as he started toward the deck. "Why don't we take off our shoes and walk barefoot in the grass. What say we have a picnic at the British Museum?"

"If you mean a picnic with real food," I drooled hungrily, "I'm game."

George Stedders, true to his duty as officer of the day, accompanied us to the gangplank. Lacking a search warrant, we walked right past Drummond's cabin without more than a casual peek through the porthole. Gulls glided lazily overhead screeching defiance at the waves. A ship's horn blared in the distance. And I wondered whether our suspect had murdered his best friend.

As we stepped onto the plank, Geoff turned and firmly shook the first mate's hand.

"I want you to know," he declared, "how much we appreciate your cooperation. If you keep our visit confidential we will be even more in your debt."

"You've nothin' ta worry about there," Stedders declared. "I still remember the old slogan 'LOOSE LIPS SINK SHIPS.' Anyone in particular you don't want to know?"

"As a matter of fact," I smiled, "Sam Drummond is one chap that shouldn't be troubled with the news."

"And," Weston added, "we'd appreciate your letting us know when he returns." My partner salvaged a wrinkled scrap of paper from his wallet and scribbled some figures on it. "Here's our telephone number. We'll be delighted to hear from you even at two or three in the morning. Cheerio."

At the bottom of the gangplank we waved a last farewell to the sailor standing at the rail and began our trek down the pier. Crowded tenements formed the backdrop for the station wagon awaiting us on shore.

\* \* \* \* \*

A short while later those crumbling tenements were replaced by a gigantic polished marble cube as we braked to a stop between two parked police cruisers. Evidently Twigg—methodical to the last—still had his men turning the annex upside down on the chance that only a few of the jewels had escaped. A bobby stood guard at the main entrance. And plainclothes men could be seen scurrying about the grounds with metal detectors, shovels, and sounding equipment. No doubt similar frantic efforts were taking place inside.

"Whether or not the Inspector uncovers hidden treasure," I remarked with a touch of awe, "he certainly has a shot at finding the building's flaw."

"Or," Geoff added grimly, "of proving that it hasn't any. I think he's putting together a case against poor Dodd. And unless we do something quickly, my trumped-up theory may just send an innocent man to Newgate."

"But," I objected, "surely all we have to do is show Twigg the key and the piece of tape."

Weston shook his head.

"That's not enough, John. I can hear the prosecutor now examining us on the stand. 'Are you quite sure that the key wasn't some child's toy discarded near the Queen's feet? Couldn't that Drummond fellow have found tape stuck to a hymnal or to his shoe and disposed of it as others had their gum?' When it comes right down to it, we don't have any evidence unless we discover how the jewels were smuggled out. If we don't, my theory stands and Sir Thomas is guilty by the process of elimination. But he's not. I'm sure of it."

We got out of the motorcar and began walking the cement path toward the bobby. Geoffrey's gloom had by now descended upon me.

"Perhaps," I suggested with a ray of hope, "if you tell Twigg your suspicions, he'll pick up the sailor for further questioning. Who knows, confronting the chap with even flimsy evidence might force a confession."

"It might," Geoff agreed. "It might also cause the force to be sued for harassment. The Inspector isn't going to lift a finger against the man unless he has a rattling good case. What we do, of course, is another matter entirely."

By now I recognized the stoic figure standing in front of us. Underneath that black helmet brim was Tracy Sloan! At almost the same instant he made us out and formed a megaphone of his hands.

"Well, Well! Weston and Taylor! Up to your old tricks, I see. Good to have you with us."

"And good to be here," Weston shouted in reply. "With you around, nothing disappears without a Trace!"

I groaned.

"One of these days," I warned out of the side of my mouth, "old Taylor will collapse from all that PUNishment. Please, not on an empty stomach!"

"If you do," Geoff smiled broadly, "I'll revive you with a PUNgent odor."

Double groan. It doesn't do the slightest good to protest my partner's sense of humor. Protests have a habit of turning into contests. Resisting a try at one-up-man-ship, I called to our friend. By this time he was near enough so it wasn't necessary to split my vocal chords.

"Is Inspector Twigg around? We have some urgent business with him."

"Just a minute." Sloan unclipped a walkie-talkie from his belt, and spoke into it briefly. Returning it to his hip, he addressed us again. "The Inspector should be out here shortly. Meanwhile he says that you two should make yourselves at home."

"Marvelous," I enthused. "Where are the beach parasols and lemonade?"

"I'm afraid we're out of those," Tracy retorted with a grin. On our arrival he extended us his hand. "But you'll find some shade in the vestibule."

"And where," Geoff asked in a businesslike tone, "is the air conditioner?"

"The air conditioner?" Sloan seemed puzzled. "There's no air conditioning in the vestibule, if that's what you—"

"I mean," my colleague broke in, "what I said. I want to examine this establishment's cooling unit."

Tracy's expression cleared.

"Oh, that! It's over on the east side in a cut in the embankment."

"Thank you." My colleague bowed his head slightly in appreciation for the tidbit. "You may tell Twigg when he arrives that he'll find us over there. You might also mention that white uniforms would be more appropriate for the summer. Step inside yourself, man, before you drop from the heat."

"I wish I could, sir," Sloan replied with feeling.

We left the bobby still standing in the sunlight and began skirting the edge of the building. My eyes followed as the wall—slab-by-slab—fit together with alarming precision. There was no loose cement or sloppy workmanship. The place was, indeed, a fortress. And that impression was heightened by the condition of the lawn. A shrub leaned over in wilting disgrace—its roots exposed to the air. Here and there the grass was pocked with ugly holes where Twigg's men had vented their spleen on buried beverage cans. We were treading through what looked very much like a half-exploded mine field.

"A sorry place for a picnic," Geoffrey lamented. "Too many gophers. My word, Taylor! Look over there. If it isn't Victoria Falls in miniature!"

But I'd already seen it. A tall grey box hugging the wall was spewing forth a cascade of sparkling water that plummeted from fin to fin until landing in a reflecting pool two stories below. We had found our air-conditioning unit.

"Incredible!" I marvelled. "I had no idea one could extract that much humidity from the air! I presume this means we'll be getting our feet wet."

"Quite so." Weston eyed the structure from top to bottom. "There's an access panel on the side that I want a peek behind. Roll up your trouser legs and plunge right in. Cool water will do wonders for your feet."

We took off our shoes and stepped gingerly into the pond. Gravel at the bottom was rounded and safe, so we had little difficulty reaching and removing the panel. Geoff leaned inside and started studying the works. Just then Twigg cleared his throat to announce his arrival at the edge of the moat.

"Who'd believe it? Weston and Taylor in knickers! Good show, fellows, but there's no way into the ducts from here. We've already established that. No trained monkey scampering out with the diamonds, I'm afraid. And, furthermore, with white uniforms the constabulary would resemble ice cream vendors."

"Which," Weston quipped while turning to face him, "would no doubt do wonders for public relations. Wait a second and we'll join you on dry land."

I could tell that underneath the bravado, my partner was disappointed and slightly embarrassed. He must have been banking heavily on the air conditioning as a solution. As we waded ashore I could almost see his mind shift gears, change directions, and start accelerating all over again. We climbed out into the grass, bent over, and went through the routine of squeezing into sticky socks and tightening our shoelaces.

"Inspector," Geoff complimented seriously, "you're beginning to cultivate imagination. Congratulations. Now if you'd only add faith to that, you'd be a master in your field."

"I was not aware," Twigg responded dryly, "that being 'born again' heightened one's detective abilities. You, for one, don't seem very hot on the trail at the moment."

"Quite true," I admitted, "but we are still confident of God's guidance in our lives. And that means we may be more relaxed while examining clues."

"Or may not be," Twigg noted skeptically. "I've seen Weston pace a hole in his carpet more than once."

Geoff tied his shoe and regained his feet.

"It's useless, John, to debate with an opponent

as wiley and clever as the Inspector. He sees all of our human frailties with the eye of a professional. And he's determined never to be human himself and acknowledge his need for repentance. As Shaw would say, he's a superman—a veritable keg of dynamite bent upon—"

"That will be enough!" Twigg interrupted. "You've made your point. Now what's this about 'urgent business' you have with me?"

"We've come for an exchange of information," Weston informed him.

The Scotland Yarder eyed us shrewdly.

"Which means," he translated, "that you're jolly well at loose ends. But I don't mind. Let's exchange. I'm grateful to you two blokes for handing me the thief on a silver platter so to speak."

"Then," I ventured, "you've got more evidence against Sir Thomas."

"Almost enough to bring him in," Twigg nodded. "We checked those door motors. The front entrance, it turns out, opens fastest—which means the other doors were never even ajar. And we've found no way out of the building. What's more, there's the matter of some gambling debts that have turned up. Dodd wouldn't be the first man led into crime by his own intemperance. Now what revelations do you have?"

My partner put his hand in his pocket and extracted two envelopes.

"We have," he admitted ruefully, "these. The first is the remains of what may have been a plastic key. We found it in the Queen's ashes. The second is a tape with two fingerprints on it—probably

Drummond's—that was stuck to the bottom of a pew at St. Albans. I believe Sam was paid off today for his part in the theft."

"That's nice." Twigg's smile was infectious but not very encouraging as he accepted the envelopes. "We'll check the prints and let you know if they match. But I don't think you've got much. Please tell me when you've figured out how Drummond managed the robbery. Now if you two gentlemen will excuse me, I've got other business."

"I've noticed." Weston surveyed the grounds. "Now I finally know why you fellows call yourselves the 'Yard.' Do landscaping on the side, don't you?" He gestured with his hands. "What style is this? 'Early Battle of Britain?' "

"We don't waste our time thinking up names," the Inspector replied bluntly. "We just do our job. Have a wonderful afternoon. And if you feel like another swim, go right ahead." He turned on his heels and walked briskly towards the front of the annex. A few strides away he started whistling.

"Now there," I remarked, "goes a confident man."

"And," Geoff added, "he would seem to have every reason for cockiness. He's more efficient than I gave him credit for. And we are a couple of bunglers. If there's anything here, Twigg will find it. Let's toddle home for supper. Maybe a few bites of food will clear up our thinking."

* * * * *

The tingle of the shower was refreshing. Grit and perspiration washed away. And so did the feeling of frustration—almost. I was a new man as

I walked down the hall towards the aroma escaping from the kitchen. Geoff had decided to take his mind off the day's misadventures by trying his hand at the culinary art. Had it been up to me we'd have been supping on salad and gelatin with an iced lolly for dessert. But Geoff didn't seem to mind the cooker. When I strolled into the room the window fan was on high and so were three burners. I breathed deeply to sample the air.

"My dear Weston," I ventured with surprise, "surely that couldn't be roast grouse!"

My partner picked a pot off the fire and scooped out three heaping portions of stuffed onions swimming in some sort of sauce.

"And why not," he smiled in anticipation. "We haven't had anything wild in months. Grouse, peas and cheese pudding! I can't think of a more delightful meal, can you?"

"Indeed not," I agreed. "But make my portion a small one. And speaking of portions, who's going to be joining us?"

"Oh, that. I've set an extra place for Sir Thomas. He called while you were sprucing up—seemed very serious about wanting to speak with us. So I took the liberty of inviting him over. He should be here any minute now. Be a good chap and try your hand with the fly swatter, will you, while I put the food out."

"With pleasure." I picked my weapon from a nail by the icebox and searched the area around the cat's dish for prey. "While we're waiting," I added, "there's one question I've been meaning to ask you."

Weston opened the oven and pulled out the birds.

"Ask away," he invited.

"Well, how did you know this afternoon that neither the captain nor Drummond were on board?"

"The first was elementary really." Geoff hefted the pan from the oven to the table. "Tiny hardly would have spoken about the captain as he did if the man were anywhere within hearing distance. And as for Drummond, well he simply couldn't have been on the ship. I looked for Twigg's operative as we approached the pier and he was missing. So Sam was somewhere else. I might have missed the Yarder but . . . "

The doorbell sounded—heralding the arrival of our dinner guest.

"Excuse me." Weston put down the pan and shed his pot holders. "I'll be back in half a dozen swats." He disappeared in the direction of the living room only to reappear in a moment with our distinguished visitor.

Sir Thomas Dodd was almost as I remembered him. He was impeccably dressed in a brown tweed. His full face, however, showed the strain of the last twenty-four hours. His shoulders drooped slightly and his hand, as he extended it, was not the bundle of energy that it had once been.

"A very good evening, Mr. Taylor. It's so nice of you to have me."

"Not at all. Not at all." I grasped his hand and

wondered what to do with the fly swatter. "We were very impressed by you last night, actually. I've wanted to make your acquaintance under more . . . auspicious conditions. Have a seat." I gestured with a nod toward the nearest chair. "We can talk while we're eating. Do you like grape juice?"

"Yes, of course. With ice, please."

He took his place at the table while I approached the refrigerator, hung the swatter back on its hook, and returned with a bottle of juice and a tray of ice. Meanwhile Geoff was serving out the last vegetable.

"This," Sir Thomas declared as we finished preparations, "certainly is quaint. You fellows aren't slaves to social convention. I like that."

"What's more," Geoff added tongue-in-cheek, "we possess neither dining room nor tablecloth. And the maid sets foot inside only once a month." He plopped the shakers down between the peas and onions. Everything now being ready, we pulled out chairs and joined our guest.

"It's our custom," I explained to Sir Thomas, "to begin each meal with prayer. Geoffrey, will you lead us?"

"Certainly." He bowed his head as Dodd looked on in bemusement.

"Father, you've given us an exquisite lesson in humility today. Thanks for that. And thank you also for bringing this friend here tonight. Please guide our conversation around this table. There's also the matter of Twigg—your proof to us that man can't be argued into repentance. We beg you to soften and burden his heart through your Spirit.

Lord, bring him into your family. We want you to know as well how grateful we are for today's sunshine, for the crops that have prospered, and for giving us food in this world filled with famine. We love you. In Jesus' name we offer thanks and praise. Amen."

Sir Thomas stuck his fork into a stuffed onion and chopped off a piece.

"That," he declared, "was a beautiful prayer."

"No, it wasn't," my colleague disagreed. "It was merely a chat with my best friend." He picked up a carving knife and started to work on the larger of the birds. "Would you care for breast or drumstick? Perhaps some wild rice stuffing?"

"A little of each, actually."

Geoff began doling out generous pieces onto our plates. Dodd took a tentative bite or two but seemed somewhat preoccupied.

"No doubt," I guessed aloud, "the Inspector told you this afternoon that we believe you innocent. Is that why you've stopped by?"

Our guest reddened slightly and speared a piece of meat with his fork.

"As a matter of fact, it's not. I have neither come to plead, pay, cajole, nor pump for information. Don't believe in it. I simply wish to make a report and to pursue an allusion that your partner made last night."

"Your report," Geoff broke in suavely, "is probably about the showcases. Did you find anything amiss?"

"Unfortunately, no. But you were right about one thing."

"What's that?"

Sir Thomas smiled with bitter satisfaction.

"The Inspector's men hadn't checked them."

"And what," I inquired between bites, "was the allusion?"

He looked from the one to the other of us for a long moment before answering.

"Actually it was your mention of Tyndale. You said something about his room containing the answer to the greatest mystery of all. What did you mean by that?"

My partner savored a piece of grouse and leaned forward, gesturing with his fork.

"I meant that this fellow Tyndale made a revolutionary discovery. You're familiar, of course, with his story. He translated the Bible into English and for that was virtually banished to the continent. He continued to write pieces like *The Parable of the Wicked Mammon* and for that was declared a heretic, defrocked, strangled and burned. He sealed his own fate because he had stumbled upon something more important than station, honor, employment or life itself."

"You're referring then," Dodd concluded, "to the doctrine of justification by faith."

"In part," Geoff agreed. "But those theological terms sound so prim and stiff. I'm talking about something that boggles the imagination. Tyndale discovered why he was here! Why he lived and breathed and ate and slept. He learned that he had ultimate meaning. He learned . . . to be happy and satisfied. To him the gospel meant—I believe these were his words—'good, merry, glad and joyful tidings that make a man's heart glad and make him sing, dance, and leap for joy.' Now that's something worth living *and dying* for! He had been blind. But he embraced Jesus as his Savior, and saw new horizons never before dreamed of."

"That," I pointed out to Dodd, "is the essence of Christianity. You know the doctrines: Christ died to pay for sins, and salvation is a free gift to those who repent and believe in Him. But Tyndale did more than mouth creeds. He actually surrendered his life in trust to the Son of God who'd loved him enough to be crucified in his place!"

"You're saying then," Sir Thomas suggested with some uneasiness, "that I'm not a Christian."

Geoffrey drank deeply from his grape juice.

"I'm saying nothing of the kind. You are, after all, the only one who can see inside yourself. But if God is merely some abstract concept to you, then yes. Christianity is much more than that! Sir Thomas, you might well lose your job, your standing in the community, and even your freedom. If that happens, will God's Spirit sustain you as He did Tyndale?"

Dodd thought for a moment.

"I can't honestly say that He will." He cleared his throat. "But I'm not about to get down on my knees and plead for mercy in front of you chaps. Haven't come here to gain your sympathy, you know. Just wanted a couple of answers."

"I quite understand," Geoffrey nodded sympathetically. "It's a very personal matter. Why don't you do some reading in John, Romans, and the Book of Acts? Then when you're ready, talk matters over with the Lord. Be open and honest with . . ."

The telephone jangled in the other room and Geoff glanced hopefully in my direction.

"Pardon me," I wiped my lips with a napkin. "You fellows keep right on chatting. Just don't gobble up all the pudding."

I hurried to the living room and pounced on the receiver before the ringing stopped.

"Hallo. Sleuths, Limited. May I be of help?"

"Not likely. But I'd be 'appy to 'elp you." The tinny voice at the other end belonged to Tiny Stedders.

"Good show!" I exclaimed. "So Drummond's finally coming back home."

" 'e 'as. And ya woulda 'eard about it sooner, but I couldn't get to a telephone. Ate 'is dinner, 'e 'as, an' gone to 'is cabin. It's passin' strange, too. 'e's usually in a pub 'til late."

I did some quick mental figuring.

"Thanks for calling, Tiny. We'll try to get there in about forty-five minutes."

"You'd better," he warned, "or the bloke 'ill be asleep. Cheerio."

"And good day to you."

I hung up and strolled back into the kitchen. By then Geoff and Sir Thomas had concluded their conversation and were engaged in some serious eating. Their plates, in fact, were showing serious signs of emptiness. I sat down and joined in.

"That," I informed my partner between chews, "was from the King Richard. I fear we shall have to make a quick end to our meal."

# CHAPTER 5

## *The Breathless Grin*

Light gleamed from several portholes aboard the King Richard and one lone bulb attracted bugs halfway down the pier. But other than that the night pressed in like a shroud—surrounding us with blackness. I hesitated before slamming the station wagon door—unwilling to lose even the soft glimmer of the overhead lamp. Geoff pointed to the faint outline of a motorcar across the road.

"That," he spoke in a subdued tone, "must be the shadow."

"He certainly looks dark enough for the job," I agreed. "Why don't we shuffle on over and say hello. The fellow must be about ready to scream from boredom."

"Why not?" Weston took a torch out of his pocket. "Let's turn the tables and have a little fun at the Yard's expense."

We felt our way to the other side of the

street—our feet making hardly a sound on the cobblestones. Then we followed the curb to the rear of the police cruiser. Geoff carefully made his way to the side window away from the pier. He aimed his torch inside and switched it on.

"That will be enough loitering there, mate," he boomed with authority. "Let me see some identification."

The detective jumped as though he'd been shot and turned his head only to be blinded by the torch. One hand slid automatically into his pocket in search of a badge. He opened his mouth to speak and only then recognized Weston.

"Great Scott! You nearly scared me out of a year's life. What is the idea sneaking up on a man like that?"

"Why," Geoffrey laughed, "I thought that was standard police procedure when investigating parked motorcars. You're looking alert, Peterson. Night work must agree with you."

"Alert, he says! If you two had seen me before you shined that light in my face, you wouldn't think so. I worked all morning, and now here I am back for the graveyard shift! And this a Sunday!"

"That's a ruddy shame," my partner agreed. "But at least you were able to attend church."

"And," Peterson complained, "I should have been paid double for that! I've never heard such inane twaddle. It's easier keeping my eyes open here."

"Tell me," I broke in, "you didn't happen to notice who was sitting in front of Drummond, did you?"

"In church?"

"Yes."

The detective unconsciously rubbed his chin.

"I can't say for sure. . . . But I believe it was an old lady. Yes. As I recall she was wearing a scarf or shawl or the like. And she had on a baggy dress."

"You're sure," Weston prompted, "that it was a lady?"

"Either that," the detective amended warily, "or a man dressed up like one."

My partner fished a bag of peanuts from his pocket and tossed them in the Yarder's lap.

"Here's something to munch on while you wait. Any excitement lately?"

"Oh, things have really been frantic. A sailor left about an hour ago, then went back aboard a few moments later. That's the only movement since Drummond brought me here."

"Well, keep on your toes," Weston advised. "We're going to try to shake Sam up a bit. If he leaves after our little talk, I'd be very interested in knowing whom he meets. So would the Yard. Good day, Peterson."

"Good evening, and the best of luck to you. Thanks for the nuts."

As we walked out onto the pier, inky waters below lapped impatiently at the pilings. There was no moon, and the ship ahead looked all but deserted. More to hear a voice than anything else, I tapped Weston on the shoulder and half whispered a complaint.

"I say, that was a rather mean trick to play on

Alfred. The poor fellow might have bumped his head."

"I suppose so," Geoffrey admitted, "But I needed him wide awake."

"He certainly is that," I chuckled. "Now the question is, will Drummond be?"

"We'll soon find out, won't we."

Geoff stepped onto the gangplank and began a rapid ascent. I followed. Within seconds we were standing on the deck and looking around for a sign of life. We didn't have long to wait. A silhouette glided out of the shadows and came toward us.

"Been waitin' for you," Tiny growled. "You'll need an escort to the cabin or the cap'n just might throw ya to the fish. But don't let Sam know I told ya to come. I'd never 'ear the last o' it."

"Don't worry," Geoff assured him. "We won't. Lead on, McDuff."

"The name's Stedders."

"Yes, of course."

Our parade passed a lighted room and several darkened chambers before stopping at the diver's door. I couldn't hear any sounds inside, but the eighth-inch steel plate could have muffled them. A light shone through the porthole. We had evidently caught our suspect before he'd retired. Tiny did the honors—pounding the door with one of his ham-like fists.

"Look alive there, mate. You've got a couple o' visitors!"

There was only silence. Nothing stirred.

"Open the door and be sociable! I tell you ya got a couple a gentlemen out 'ere."

Again there was only the rustle of breeze and the murmur of waves striking the side of the ship. Weston stepped over to the porthole and pressed his face to the glass.

"You needn't shout anymore," he concluded gravely. "I'm afraid Sam is far beyond looking alive. Go tell the captain he has a murder on board. And there's a Scotland Yard detective in a motorcar at the end of the pier. You'd better fetch him."

"You mean 'e's—"

"Yes, yes. He's dead, man. Get a move on."

The sailor peered curiously through the port-hole, shuddered, and hurried off—leaving us alone for the moment in front of the door. I took out my gloves and slid them on.

"I presume we're going inside."

My partner squeezed his own fingers into a pair and nodded.

"We are. And there won't be much time, so make the most of it."

He jerked the latch and opened the door wide with a clang. The place reeked with the sour smell of vomit. Sam Drummond was lying sprawled on the bed—staring at us with unblinking eyes and an evil grin. He seemed as unfriendly in death as he had been in life. Weston walked over and felt the corpse's neck.

"He's been dead for at least an hour, John. The body's already cold and rigor mortis is starting to set in. An autopsy will have to affix the exact time, of course. But I imagine he was already dead when Tiny called us."

"What do you suppose killed him?"

"Probably arsenic," Weston considered. "Notice how tight the muscles are. And there's some slight hemorrhaging. But we're wasting time. Do you see that water on the floor by the sink? Sop it up with a paper towel and seal it in plastic. Then look for the poison. I'm going to see if I can find the pay-off money."

"With pleasure. Amazing the water didn't all evaporate. It's rather stuffy in here."

"Yes, isn't it." Geoff was already going through the dead man's pockets.

I stooped down and soaked up part of the puddle. Twigg's men could have the rest. With the towel safely bagged, I next turned my attention to a snack table in the corner. It was the only piece of furniture that wasn't an exact replica of what we'd found earlier in O'Brian's room. Judging from the containers on the table, Sam had favored coffee, tea, ale and bouillon. The ale sported a 'Wild Boar' label.

"We've found our fire-bomb thrower," I reported. "The fellow collected the bottles."

"Not a very bright hobby," my partner answered over his shoulder. "He doesn't seem to have the money. But I haven't tried his shoes yet. Anything unusual in the jars?"

I opened each in turn—sniffing at their contents and examining the granules through my lens.

"There doesn't seem to be anything added," I concluded at length. "It's just ordinary coffee, tea and bouillon. And there's precious little of the latter. He must have used the stuff as salt tablets."

I removed the lid of the coffee pot and looked inside. It was empty.

"He might have been poisoned at mess," I suggested. "That would explain the early retiring—stomach cramps, you know."

"Perhaps." Geoff opened the locker and started poking around inside. "But perhaps not. What's in the sink?"

I walked on over and viewed the smelly mixture with distaste.

"Partially digested food, of course. Oh, I see what you mean. I'd say it looks a little too well digested. The arsenic may have been administered after the meal. And that means . . . " I snapped my fingers. "There's only one other place it could be."

I unscrewed the cap to the toothpaste and squeezed out a mite. The stuff looked normal. It smelled normal. And I wasn't about to taste it.

"There's no proof as yet," I admitted. "But this tube probably contains your poison. The mint would mask any odor or bad flavor and a potent formula could be absorbed directly through the mouth membrane."

"Excellent deduction, Taylor. We'll advise the Yard to make some tests." Geoff closed the locker and surveyed the room with an eye for detail. "The money doesn't seem to be in evidence. That, of course, provides us with a possible motive. There's nothing else we can do here. Let's head outside before incensed sailors stampede through the door like a herd of elephants. Come to think of it, someone should have arrived by now. Tiny must have gone after Peterson first instead of the captain."

We walked back out on deck and turned to secure the hatch. Then the whole ship lit up like a Christmas tree. The captain had evidently been informed of the crime. I blinked at the glare and gazed forward just in time to see a group of men bearing down on us. The Scotland Yarder was trotting out in front with coattails flying.

"Hold on there," Weston commanded sternly. "Drummond isn't going anywhere. And it won't help matters if someone trips and breaks a leg."

Realizing the truth of the statement, Peterson slowed. But he was still out of breath as he reached us.

"What," he panted, "do we have here?"

The others—four in all—gathered around us as we blocked the entrance. They were big-muscled men of differing heights but with a common concern.

"We have," Geoffrey announced, "a very ugly poisoning. Arsenic—probably injected into the toothpaste. And there may be a large sum of money missing. I suggest that everyone stay aboard ship at least for the time being. And stand back from the cabin, please. If you want to see, look through the porthole."

"That's right," Peterson took his cue. "Everyone keep your distance. The laboratory chaps will be here any moment, and we've got to preserve the evidence."

"Blimey," one of the seamen muttered, "at least it wasn't in his food. You'd have thrown me in the brig for sure." He was a heavyset fellow— evidently the cook.

"It would do you good," a companion jibed. "A month on bread and water and you'd be rid of that double chin of yours."

"Very funny. Very funny. You ought to be a clown in the—"

"That will be quite enough," the detective ordered. "We're not here to bicker. Take one look through the porthole and then return to whatever you were doing before."

"Might I suggest," Geoffrey interceded, "that the men should be kept together at least until help arrives. Otherwise the murderer might dispose of the money. If it's all right with you, I could take them somewhere for questioning while you stand guard here."

"A rattling good idea," Peterson agreed. "Captain Cosgrove's still on the bridge—didn't seem particularly put out about the killing, in fact. If you march them up there you can keep an eye on him too."

By now three of the sailors—including the cook—had gone over to view the body through the glass. Tiny, who had no desire for a second look, gave full attention to what we were saying.

"If you ask me," he chimed in, "it was the cap'n what murdered 'im. They was always arguin' 'bout somethin'. An' now 'e's up there watchin' the telly—not even carin' that Sam's dead."

"You may be right," I observed. "But if I'd killed him, I'd be the first bloke down here just to keep people from thinking that."

"Mates," Weston raised his voice, "lead the way to the bridge. We're going to sit down and have a little talk about the night's events. It's my duty to inform you that everyone here is under suspicion, so cooperation is to your own advantage."

Amidst a good deal of grumbling, we left Peterson and headed toward the bow. Tiny, at my partner's request, led the way. Wally, the cook, lumbered just behind him, followed by the two sailors who must have worked the engine room. Both had traces of grease on their uniforms. The sharp-tongued chap was short and slender but had arms as thick as fence posts. He was a regular blond, blue-eyed dynamo with quick movements and an air of tirelessness. His companion seemed almost the opposite—deliberate, steady, and economical in the use of words. But from the way they were commiserating together, I could see they were fast friends. None of the men fit my image of a poisoner. I could visualize them smashing heads and breaking necks, but not adulterating dental cream.

Weston and I took the rear as we trudged up steep metal stairs toward Cosgrove's domain. I would have preferred a meeting on deck by the gangplank to keep any interloper aboard from escaping, but I didn't say anything. Geoff had evidently concluded that there was no one on the ship but the crew. With the help of the handrail I clambered up the last few steps and stood slightly out of breath on the second level. There was a hatchway in front of us and the procession was already filing through. Geoff and I followed.

The bridge was like nothing I'd ever seen before. Three or four other rooms must have had their walls cut away with a blow torch to provide the space. The floor was plush with thick, red carpet. Brass fittings glistened under indirect lighting. And maroon vinyl easy chairs and sofas were scattered at regular intervals. I half expected a bellhop to pop out of nowhere and offer to take our bags. Except for us, however, the only one present was a bushy-faced salt in a captain's uniform trying hard to watch a Barlow rerun on the telly. As the last of us pushed into the cabin, he gave up in annoyance and switched off the set.

"What's the meaning of this?" he fairly bellowed over the men's talking. "Get out of my quarters and leave me be!"

"I'm afraid we can't do that, Cosgrove." Geoff stepped forward and confronted the fellow. "Drummond's been killed, and whether you like it or not that takes precedence over some television whodunit. Sit down and we'll all have a friendly chat."

"I don't feel friendly." Cosgrove squinted suspiciously at my partner. "You're not that blighter from the Yard. Who are you anyway?"

"The name's Weston—Geoffrey Weston. And the gentleman you met has asked me to ask some questions."

"Weston . . . Weston. That sounds familiar." He relaxed somewhat. "Oh, you're the chap that always gets in the Yard's hair. I've had many a laugh reading how you make monkeys of that imperialist gestapo."

"I'm the one," Geoff smiled. "Now will you please sit down."

"Sure I'll sit down," the captain conceded in his gravelly voice. "This might be even better than what I was watching." He sank deeply into an armchair.

"And the rest of you men," my partner gestured, "take whatever seat you prefer. Sit down, quiet down, and we'll get this phase of the investigation over with just as quickly as possible."

One by one the sailors reluctantly followed the captain's example. In a matter of seconds they were seated and quieting down.

"Now," Geoffrey continued. "I already know most of you fellows. Cosgrove, I've heard a good deal about you—"

"I'll bet you have," the captain interrupted. "Most of it lies." Much to my disgust he took a pipe out of his pocket and began filling it.

"And," Weston addressed the cook, "I believe you're Wally. Tiny and I are also acquainted. That leaves two of you—"

"The sassy one," Cosgrove broke in again, "is Bobby Black. Walks like a bobby, talks like a bobby, even smells like—"

"That will be quite enough out of you," Weston ordered. "For a communist you certainly don't care very much for the working class."

"Working class, my eye. They're a bunch of ruddy capitalists, every one of them. Every time I turn my back they steal me blind!"

Geoffrey sighed.

"It appears, Mr. Cosgrove, that I'm going to get very little accomplished with the rest unless I speak with you first."

The captain lit up, leaned back, and took a puff.

"That suits me fine."

"I'm sure it does. When did you return to the ship?"

"At about seven."

"Tell me," my partner pressed, "everything you did from that moment until now."

"That's not hard," Cosgrove laughed. "I watched the telly, ate, read, walked the deck and watched the telly. What else is there to do in port?"

"You never visited with Drummond?"

"Of course not. Frankly, the man revolted me. He was decadent to the core—possessed with greed."

"You're not so pure yourself, mister," Black shot across the room. "You and your—"

"Please control yourself," Weston commanded in exasperation. "Bobby, you'll get your turn. But I want this questioning conducted in an orderly manner. Is that understood?"

"Yes, sir."

"Thank you." Geoff collected his thoughts. "Now, captain, you went on a tour of the King Richard. At what time was that?"

"At about eight. I like to take a stroll a bit after eating. It helps the digestion."

"And you didn't run across Drummond?"

"No. He must have been in his cabin."

"But," Geoff prompted, "you did walk by his door."

Cosgrove's leathery face cracked into a smile.

"That is, I believe, the only way around the ship."

"Did anyone else see you?"

"Yes. Brady over there did." He indicated the larger of the engine room workers—a young fellow with tatoos running up and down his arms.

Weston shifted his attention.

"Is that true, Brady?"

"Yes, sir. I was sitting on deck writing a letter."

"Then it was still daylight?"

"Yes. But the sun was going down."

"Thank you." Geoff now returned his gaze to the captain. "Why is it, Cosgrove, that you're a communist?"

"Do you really want to know?"

"I usually do when I ask a question."

The captain blew deliberately on his fingernails and rubbed them across his lapel.

"Well, I'll tell you. I saw some almighty lords and ladies sitting beside their swimming pools and attending all the proper social functions. And I saw myself sweating ten and twelve hours a day. It didn't seem right. And there were a whole bunch of other blokes like me—no better'n cogs in a machine. So I read *Das Kapital*. It made sense."

"That's interesting," Weston observed. "Because it sounds as though in spite of your hatred for greed, you espoused communism out of greed. 'Someone else has what I want, so I'll take it.' "

The captain shifted in his chair.

"It's not that way at all," he protested. "Those capitalist scabs, they're the selfish ones. They took what was rightfully mine. And they've been holding us all down in order to—"

"I quite understand," Weston interrupted sarcastically. "You are a part of the downtrodden masses. Poppycock! In the nineteenth century there might have been some legitimacy to your complaint—back when everyone slaved long hours in a factory without sick leave or retirement. But today the unions have enough power to bleed the companies. Your argument's so much bilgewater."

"Says you." Cosgrove puffed on his pipe, then held it aloft in his best professional style. "But when we're in power, you'll sing a different tune. And we *will* come to power. History's flow is on our side."

Geoff eyed the captain gravely.

"You amaze me. In one breath you speak of giving liberty to cogs. In the next you subject us all to some dispassionate, unalterable stream. In order to 'free' man you turn him into a mere animal manipulated by economic forces."

"You chaps," the captain disagreed, "may be

manipulated, but we socialists conform ourselves with the economic laws that govern history. In that, old boy, lies our freedom."

Geoff slapped his forehead.

"Oh, brother! You remind me of a swimmer caught in the current who starts swimming toward the falls so he'll be liberated from the current. He'll be liberated all right. He'll break his fool neck. I can never quite understand determinists like you. What's the rationality of fatalism, anyway?"

"Fatalism!" Cosgrove was incensed. "I'd hardly call it that. I'm not popping over any falls, Weston. I'm heading for a paradise—a world free from poverty and war. Humanity itself will be regenerated once the filthy disease of capitalism has been eradicated."

"The disease of capitalism!" My partner pointed emphatically to every person in the room except the captain. "There. There. There. There. There's your 'disease of capitalism.' You're not talking about some mindless bacteria, man. You're talking about brainwashing and killing billions of people in search of some unproven and unprovable dream. 'Kill the last capitalist and wars will cease.' Do you really believe that? Look at the war between China and Vietnam. What does that do to your theory? Or the war between Vietnam and its other communist neighbors? Or the border skirmishes between China and the U.S.S.R.? Can you really swallow the argument that capitalism has somehow caused those conflicts? It isn't capitalism that's the problem, captain. It's sin. There's a rottenness in man—every man—that impels him to destructiveness. You dream of some economic paradise, but you can't change hearts! Only Christ can do that. And only He can produce a utopia."

"I knew it!" Cosgrove slammed his fist down on the arm of his chair. "You're bonkers—a blinkin' religious fanatic! Don't you see you're being manipulated by the establishment? Defend the status quo. Wait in line for your phony 'pie in the sky.' But you won't get it! The merchants and bishops are laughing up their sleeves at you . . . laughing all the way to the bank!"

Geoffrey shook his head sadly.

"I feel like I'm listening to a propaganda record. But then totalitarianism systems seldom spark originality. Oh," he raised his hand in protest, "I know you'll claim that when utopia is reached governments will wither away. But that's more mere speculation. You intimate religion is an instrument of bourgeoisie greed. But the only truly unselfish people I know, sir, are Christians—yes, even Christian preachers. Is there such a thing as an unselfish exploiter? I read once about a communal Christian group that managed to survive in China after the takeover. They prayed and sang hymns at church while making clothes to give to the needy. They tithed one hundred percent of their food to feed the poor—keeping themselves alive by foraging for roots. And when communist leaders came to make inspections, they marveled that there were no locks on the doors. Why didn't these Christian chaps have problems with theft like the atheistic bureaucrats were experiencing?

I'll tell you why. Because Jesus Christ gives pie on the earth! He changes lives. He actually conquers greed. You, on the other hand, exploit greed to gain converts. Then you lord it over those converts like the self-serving pigs in Orwell's *Animal Farm*! And YOU offer pie in some unreachable future."

"Unreachable!" Cosgrove thundered. "We're reaching it. Hardly a month goes by when some new country doesn't come over into our camp. You blighters are on the losing side. Common sense says as much."

"Yes," Weston sighed, "you are taking over the world. And perhaps God is permitting it because the 'Christian nations' are rejecting their spiritual roots. But you'll never reach your utopia—even if you swallow up the entire earth and exterminate billions. You can't because there's no utopia in you. Greed, my friend—good old communist greed—will continue to pop up. And if you label *that* as capitalism and deal with it, you'll depopulate the world. The last man left will put down his smoking machine gun and shout to the horizon: 'At last the perfect world! And I own it all!'"

The captain's pipe went out. He paused to relight it before replying.

"You," he resumed at length, "are the most dangerous sort of bloke. You speak gibberish but manage to make it sound convincing. What you've done, of course, is to paint an even gloomier picture of man than you accuse me of producing. Man, my dear fellow, is perfectable. And we have seen some steps in that direction in the people's republics. Under capitalism, for example, millions starved in China. Now there is sufficient food."

"Let me amend that," Geoff disagreed. "Under anarchy there was starvation. Under dictatorship there is bare subsistence, forced family planning and death for 'the ugly weeds that show their heads.' And it's still a nation of greed. Why don't we use your own life as a test of communism's ability to change the heart? You *own* this ship. You *pay* wages—low wages. It would seem to me, mate, that you are an exploiter."

Cosgrove jumped to his feet.

"Preposterous!" He waved his fist in Weston's face. "Why should I give anything to a bunch of bloomin' capitalists! They'd just use it for more decadence. As long as they only get what they need, they don't exploit. And I have more to use for the cause!"

"It seems to me," my partner commented dryly, "that as long as you own this ship you have no cause. But we were talking about your life as an example of the socialist heart, weren't we? What do I know about you from our brief encounter?" Weston began counting off on his fingers. "I know you care more about television than people. I know you want money for 'the cause.' And I perceive that you hate your crew and aren't in the least concerned about Drummond's death. Furthermore, you theoretically condone murder as a method of purifying civilization. That, sir, makes you a leading candidate for Dartmoor. Sam Drummond had money—a lot. You looked in his porthole perhaps as you were walking by. You saw him counting his loot. What would prevent you from killing him to steal it? Nothing that I can think of!"

It looked for a moment as if Cosgrove was going to strike my colleague. His arm went back, and I could read the desire in his eyes. But instead he reared back and threw his pipe across the room—smashing it to pieces against the bulkhead.

"You'll pay for saying that!" he screamed. "There's a law in this country against slander. I'm going to sue you for every cent you've got."

"Spoken," Geoffrey smiled, "like a true communist. Would you like my shoe so you can rap it on my knuckles for emphasis?"

"You . . . You! . . . " The captain clenched his fists, thought better of it, and stormed out of the cabin. As his figure receded through the hatch, Weston got off a final volley.

"Don't go far," he warned. "Remember, you're a suspect."

The cabin broke into pandemonium.

"You sure give 'im 'is what for!"

"Blimey, he got run off his own."

"You coulda sold me a ticket."

"Old Pinchpenny finally got his comeuppance!"

"Coulda done it, too. Wouldn't put it past . . . "

Geoffrey waited for the noise to level off and then raised his arms for silence.

"Gentlemen. Gentlemen. I appreciate your feelings. But let's get back to business, shall we?

With the captain gone I believe we can expedite the questioning."

He gazed in turn at each member of the crew—finally stopping at the blond giant, Brady. "Mate, what did you do after it was too dark to write?"

"Why, I went to Bobby's cabin and me and him tried our hand at checkers. Then we came up here for some television. The captain lets us do that sometimes. We was all up here until Tiny came with that detective fellow."

"I see," Weston frowned. "You arrived on the bridge at what time?"

"It coulda been around nine o'clock."

"When did you eat?"

"At seven. We finished around half past."

Geoff stroked his goatee.

"Then you wrote letters for an entire hour?"

"Yes, sir." Brady's face was clear and untroubled.

Weston shifted his attention to the red-bearded first mate.

"Mr. Stedders, what were you doing between mess and eight-thirty?"

"Why, I was 'elpin' Wally 'ere in the galley. Cleanin' up. Left a little before 'e finished, though. 'ad a telephone call ta make."

"Quite so." Geoffrey pulled a bag of peanuts out of his pocket and ripped open the cellophane. "That would seem to account for you, Wally, as well. Did you go directly from the galley to the bridge?"

"Yes, sir, except for a stop at the head."

"Then you arrived before the captain got back from his walk?"

The cook shifted uneasily as folds of flesh around his middle protested the prolonged sitting position.

"Yes, sir."

"What time did he arrive?"

"I don't rightly know. But the program was 'alf over. It musta been about fifteen minutes after me."

My partner nodded thoughtfully and popped some nuts into his mouth.

"Thank you. Now that leaves only two more questions. Tiny, do you use single or double scuba tanks on this ship?"

"Double."

"I thought as much." Weston now turned toward Black. "We seem to have accounted for everyone's movements except yours. What were you doing between mess and checkers?"

The sailor ran grease-stained fingers through his unruly shock of hair.

"You may not believe this," he confessed in a nasal tone, " 'cause I ain't got witnesses, but I was taking a nap."

"I don't see why I shouldn't believe you," Geoffrey replied. "That, gentlemen, concludes the questioning. I would appreciate your staying here for a few moments until the Yard gets around to paying you a visit. My colleague and I have other pressing business, so we'll be taking leave of you now."

Weston and I pushed ourselves out of the mushy chairs and the sailors did likewise. We shook hands all around and were about to step out of the door when Geoff snapped his fingers. Something had evidently jogged his memory. He crooked his forefinger at Tiny and the two went into a huddle in a corner of the cabin away from the rest of us. Judging from the emphatic head shaking, my partner was trying to convince Stedders to do something he didn't relish. At length the mate opened a drawer to the chart table and extracted a tube of rolled-up paper. Weston accepted the tube, shook hands warmly, and rejoined me at the door.

"What," I asked as we stepped out of the cabin, "was that all about?"

Geoff crushed the tube and stuffed it in his back pocket. "Oh, nothing much. I was just getting a sight-seeing map. We're going on a fishing trip tonight—to Malta." He put his hand on the rails and started briskly down the steps.

"But," I protested as I scampered after him, "that's impossible. We don't have any reservations. And what about the investigation here?"

"The investigation here," my partner stated with finality, "is concluded. There are only two lines of the puzzle yet to be filled in—one here and one in Malta. When you're stuck in one direction on a crossword puzzle, John, what do you do?"

"Try the other direction, I suppose."

"Precisely." He landed on the deck and kept walking at top speed toward the gangplank. "And that's exactly what we're going to do. Well, well, look at that. It seems our dear captain has been apprehended trying to go ashore. How unfortunate! Quite possibly they found some money on him. I thought the Yard would have things sealed off by the time he made his little exit."

Captain Cosgrove was indeed being escorted up the gangplank by two uniformed bobbies. And, judging from his struggles and curses, he was none too happy. Just behind him in the shadows a heavyset gentleman was ascending the plank—unperturbed at the outbursts.

"Why," I called out, "if it isn't Inspector Twigg! We're running into you everywhere."

As Cosgrove was being aided aft, Twigg reached the deck and paused to wait for us. He was clearly content with the world.

"For some strange reason," he remarked, "you seem to inspire instant distaste, Geoff old bean. That fellow over there claims he was hurrying away to find an advocate so he could sue you. Wouldn't know anything about it, would you?"

My partner reached out and heartily shook the Inspector's hand.

"As a matter of fact," he admitted jovially, "I do. The fellow had the temerity to call Scotland Yard an 'imperialist gestapo.' Now I could hardly let that go by without offering a little constructive criticism, could I?"

"Hardly," Twigg grinned—slapping Weston on the back. "But I do hope you watched your words. He did seem rather serious in his threat."

"I believe I simply asked a question and offered an opinion. Nothing libelous in that. What's the latest? You didn't find any money on the captain, did you?"

The Inspector wiped his brow and loosened his tie.

"Dreadfully muggy out here on the water. No, I wasn't aware a search was in order, but we'll get right on it. I take it you think this Drummond killing is connected with a robbery."

"Very definitely," Weston agreed. "Any way you put the pieces together it has to be. Drummond picks up an envelope in church the day following a jewel theft. He returns to his ship, is poisoned, and the envelope turns up missing. That also rather strengthens my theory that the sailor, not Sir Thomas, is the thief, wouldn't you say?"

Twigg leaned on the rail and gazed ashore at a thousand lighted windows in the tenements.

"I'd like to think so," he considered aloud. "It's a messy business prosecuting a chap with a title. But the pieces can fit together another way, you know. If Dodd set fire to the dummy and that sailor bloke saw him do it, then Drummond would have a golden opportunity for blackmail. Sir Thomas—assuming for a moment there really was a payoff—then arranged to deliver the money to the church. But Sam got greedy or perhaps simply couldn't be trusted, so Dodd killed him."

"Oh, come now," Weston chided. "Surely you had Sir Thomas under surveillance. He couldn't have done all that without giving you more than supposition to go on."

"Unfortunately, he could have." The Inspector turned to face us grimly. "Because of his station, I didn't start having him followed until the morning—when it became obvious we weren't going to find any way out of the museum. Sir Thomas had plenty of time to plant the money and the poison or to hire a delivery boy and an assassin."

"Dear me," Geoff complained, "the more we try to help Dodd, the deeper he seems to sink. We're making quite a case for you, aren't we?"

"It would seem so," Twigg commented dryly. "I'm sorry I was so smug this afternoon. Actually, I'd like to prove the man innocent as much as you would. But the facts are, after all, the facts. Sir Thomas was taken into custody just after he left your lodgings."

"I see. Well then there's nothing to do but to get to work. We're going to Malta tonight. Would you care to come along?"

"To Malta! Why on earth—"

"Not on earth," Weston interrupted. "Under water. We're going to swim over the scene of another murder and ask the corpse why he was a victim."

"Well," the Inspector smiled, "I wish you luck. But right now, since my corpses don't speak, I'd best get on with the investigation. Cheerio."

"Cheerio," I echoed. "Have a nice time searching the ship."

The gangplank seemed a little longer to me as we descended. My spirits were, I suppose, a trifle low. As we walked along the pier, I noticed that Geoff, too, was lost in reflection. Sir Thomas' arrest had hit him hard. Under the single lightbulb, he paused to pick up a stone and toss it into the water. The projectile disappeared and was converted in a second into an invisible plop.

"You know," my partner observed, "sometimes I feel that's all we're doing—throwing rocks in the dark. I wonder what great uncle Sherlock would think if he could see us now."

"He'd think," I consoled, "that we're doing the best we can. That's all anybody can do. If Twigg had checked the shoe bottoms or watched Dodd from the first—"

"Don't blame him." Weston turned once again toward the shore. "We're the ones who have the answer staring us in the face but are too blind to see it. Oh, Lord, give us eyes to see and wisdom to understand. And give courage to that innocent man we've helped put behind bars. Even more than that, draw him to you."

We walked on without speaking to each other. A fog horn cried plaintively through the night. Breezes tried to blow, then faltered. And the odor of bait and dead fish—the perfume of the waterfront—tantalized our senses. As we neared the end of the pier, Geoff set aside his indecision.

"John, when we get home, I want you to run tests on that water. Check for acidity and pollutants. I want to know if it's from the tap or the river. While you're doing that, I'll call Heathrow and make reservations on the first available flight. There may also be some drawer banging necessary in order to locate our passports and visas. I believe they're still current, aren't they?"

# CHAPTER 6

## *The Island Fortress*

I pushed a button and the seat reclined to a more comfortable position. I yawned—releasing the tension built up during eighteen hours of chasing clues. The puddle was river water. The money hadn't been found. And, frankly, I didn't care anymore! All that mattered was the soft fabric behind my back and the need to close drooping eyelids. The whine of the jet engines was soothing music.

"John!" Someone shook me. "John, at least stay awake long enough to fasten your seatbelt. It won't do to have you pitch into the aisle."

"Yes . . . Of course . . . Quite right." I peeked groggily down at my lap and snapped the buckle.

The whine built to a rumble, then a dull roar. I could feel the floor under my feet vibrate. All at once we were moving and I was pressed into the cushions by the exhilarating rush of speed. I glanced out the window. Runway lights were

flashing by ever faster until they became a blur—
then disappeared below us. We were airborne.

I closed my eyes again—oblivious to anything
but the confident rumble of engines and the occasional shrillness of electric motors as the pilot
changed wing configurations.

"Excuse me." Weston leaned over me and accepted a can of orange juice from the stewardess.
"Would you like any, old boy? They've got colas
too."

"No thank you," I grumbled. "I prefer a cup
of sleep. And you could use a little of that yourself."

"I know," Geoff replied ruefully. "But as
draggy as I'll be tomorrow, thoughts are running
through my mind so fast I can't relax. I'm now certain of when the poison was planted. And Skinny
O'Brian's murder seems less mysterious every moment. But we still need to discover the link con-
necting the two deaths. The answer has to be on
board that hulk!"

"Wonderful," I groaned. "Will you please turn
off the reading lamp and think quietly in the
dark."

My partner took a New Testament out of his
shirt pocket.

"Just as soon," he assured me, "as I finish
some Bible study. Don't you find it inspiring to be
cruising up here six miles above the earth?"

"No," I stated bluntly. "I'm more inspired by
a soft bed on Baker Street and the prospect of
snoozing the cobwebs out of my mind. Good
night."

The cabin was dim except for the beam of light beside me and I was soon snoring contentedly. Every now and then a page rattled in the adjoining seat. Aside from that, there was only the gentle vibration of a bird in flight. The plane soared on through the night toward the distant commonwealth island of Malta.

* * * * *

There was a tugging at my shoulder.

"Oh, no, not again! Have a heart, Geoff. Two hours is little enough sleep for anyone. Let me have that at least!"

The shaking continued.

"You've had it, old bean. We land in three minutes. Come, have a look at the city. It's quite a show."

"Already? But it can't be . . ."

"But it is. We're banking over Fort St. Elmo right now."

I propped my eyes open and leaned toward the window for a better view. Down below, early morning sunlight glistened on the blue Mediterranean. And out at the end of a peninsula, ancient yellow walls traced an irregular pentagon on the top of a cliff. Next to the fort, but on lower ground, a city's pale brown and yellow buildings huddled together threatening to crowd out the narrow streets that formed its arteries.

"Valletta," I breathed in wonder, "looks like a ruin that forgot to get ruined."

"Doesn't it though," Weston agreed. "The town reminds me of something out of Palestine.

There's a certain timelessness about it. And notice those lines crisscrossing the countryside separating the fields. They're the reason the Nazis could never take this island. Every few hundred feet there's a stone wall. And during the war a Maltese soldier was hiding behind every one. Imagine! Only ninety-six kilometers from Sicily and the Axis was powerless against it!"

"It's harder to imagine," I reflected, "why they'd want it in the first place. That's the most desolate land I think I've ever seen."

Geoff fastened his safety belt for the landing.

"Oh, I don't know. It has a certain wild beauty. And it will look friendlier, I'm sure, after a cup of coffee."

More and more details became visible as we continued our descent. The aging dome of a cathedral separated itself from the maze. Streets bustled with activity. And outside of Valletta we could now make out wheat fields rippling in the wind. The jet skimmed over towers of approach lights, and the squeal of tires signaled our touchdown.

After disembarking, there was the usual wait at customs and then an exciting taxi ride to our hotel. Let it never be said that Maltese cabbies lag behind their Parisian counterparts in daring! When we got out at the Hotel Ancira, my right leg was weary from trying to press a nonexistent brake pedal. We pushed through a revolving door into a lobby replete with rich carpeting and potted palms. The desk clerk looked up as we approached and bared his best professional smile.

"May I help you, gentlemen?"

I leaned against the counter.

"You certainly may. We have a reservation, I believe, under the name of Weston."

The clerk flipped through his card file. "Weston . . . Weston . . . Oh, yes, here it is." He scanned pigeon holes until he'd located the key and then ceremoniously handed it to us. "Will you be staying long?"

"Until about two o'clock this afternoon."

The man's eyebrows raised a notch and his smile faltered.

"Well, you're certainly not 'sixpennies.' Enjoy what little time you have."

"Thank you," Weston assured him. "We will. And what on earth are 'sixpennies'?"

"Oh, excuse me, sir. I thought you'd know. So many of you Britishers are immigrating here to escape taxes that we've coined a word for you."

"Coined," Geoffrey noted, "in more ways than one. I assume we'll find a telephone and directory in our room."

"Yes, sir."

"Do you know of any motor launches or fishing boats that could be ready to set sail within the hour?"

The gentleman seemed puzzled.

"Fishing boats?"

"Yes, fishing boats. Small ships that people go out in when they want fish."

"Yes, of course." He cleared his throat. "But no one comes here for sport fishing."

"Good," my partner declared. "Then there should be less competition for the boats. There's a five pound note for you if you can find us something satisfactory within fifteen minutes—and another twenty-five pounds for the captain. We'll need the boat for three or four hours. Ring us up if you find anything, won't you?"

"YES, SIR." The clerk's professional courtesy was now converted to honest enthusiasm. "Is there anything else?"

"As a matter of fact," I added, "there is. Please have room service send up a pot of coffee."

Once in our room, I set to work with the telephone trying to find a sports shop with scuba gear for rent. Meanwhile, Geoff showered and changed into swim trunks and old clothes. He was going to be the day's diver. I was finally able to locate the equipment—but only for sale. Further calls proved fruitless. Then our own telephone rang. The desk clerk had a friend who had a friend. The upshot was that a certain boat in Marsamxett harbor was awaiting us. I asked him to summon a cab, and we headed downstairs. By the time we'd finished paying the clerk, there was a loud honking out front. We made a dash for the street.

As the two of us slid into the back of the taxi, I handed the driver a slip of paper.

"Take us to the city address first," I directed, "then to the harbor."

He floored the accelerator pedal and we shot out into traffic.

"Yes, sir. Anything you say."

The narrow streets were filled with motorcars—mostly small, two-liter models. And pedestrians dodged occasionally from in front of our path to squeeze onto overcrowded sidewalks. Many of the women wore large, black hoods, while their children went shirtless. Flies buzzed overhead, cockroaches crawled underfoot, and a thousand cafes along the way advertised good food and coffee.

"One might wish," I complained, "that room service had been a trifle prompter."

"I know what you mean," Weston agreed as we sped past a street vendor. "But think on the bright side. The pot will be waiting at our door when we get back. Look, there's that sporting goods store up ahead! You chaps take the scenic route around the block while I run inside."

We screeched to a halt long enough for Geoff to jump out, then turned onto what could almost be termed a boulevard. A sign warned us not to enter between seven and nine p.m. when the thoroughfare was reserved for "strolling and conversation." By the time the taxi avoided a one-way street and stopped at four traffic lights, Weston had finished with his purchases. At our arrival he was sitting on the curb surrounded by packages. I helped him load, and we headed off at a rapid pace for the harbor.

* * * * *

The captain turned out to be a man of his word. Within half an hour we were chugging down the coast at a good five knots. A pleasant northeasterly breeze flapped our shirt sleeves. Jackdaws wheeled in the sky above the cliffs. And all was well with the world. My partner broke into a whistle as he kneeled to unwrap our purchases. One by one they came into view—tanks, breathing apparatus, flippers, torch, wet suit, goggles, spear gun, and bucket.

"Now what on earth," I inquired skeptically, "do you want with that? After O'Brian's death I can understand the gun . . . but a bucket?"

Geoff assumed his best tutorial manner.

"This, my dear Taylor, is not just any bucket." He held it in front of his face. "It's a glass-bottomed pail which we shall put into the water and use as a viewer once we near the wreck. You may also find it useful for keeping track of me while I'm down among the barnacles and sturgeons."

"I think I'll be more interested in seeing the sturgeons," I kidded. "How much farther do we have to go?"

"Oh, it can't be too much longer. This whole island isn't an awfully lot bigger than London— with the suburbs included, of course. Notice those carob trees clinging to the slopes. I fancy that the shoreline's a little tamer here than a few kilometers back. The bay might be just around the next bend.

"Let's hope so," I worried. "I get seasick."

Weston hooked up the breathing apparatus and inhaled through the mouthpiece. The tanks tested full. He disrobed down to his swim trunks and tried on the wet suit. It fit like a glove. We were ready whenever the wreck was located. About that time the captain left the wheel in the hands of his son and came over. He was in his thirties—slight of build but weathered by a hundred storms.

"If your map's right," he predicted in a heavy Maltese accent, "the ship's over there." He pointed to a spot just south of us. Sure enough, I could now make out an inlet nestled in a break in the rocks. Hills around it were more gradual, and a sandy beach beckoned us to do a little swimming.

"Captain," my partner ordered, "as soon as we get abreast of the bay, be a good chap and take a sounding. Then we'll pull in a little closer to the reef."

The seaman spat on the deck.

"I've been sailing these waters for twenty years, and I don't need to take no sounding. She's fifteen fathoms on the button. We got plenty of room."

"Thank you," Geoff replied with a grin, "then we'll go directly in. Get us as close to the reef as you can without posing a danger. We'll run parallel with it for a while—using the bucket to try to spot the wreck."

"That suits me." He walked back to the wheel and took control.

As we neared shore the boat slowed and my partner leaned over the side holding the pail. We made a complete pass, and he maintained his concentration even after it was obvious we'd come up empty.

"Perhaps," I suggested, "some storm dashed

the vessel completely over the reef and into the lagoon."

"That's possible," Weston agreed while still peering into the bucket, "but it's more likely it got stuck and then floated backward at high tide. Let's make a couple more runs, and if we still don't sight anything, I'll swim over the ridge and try the other side."

The boat was midway through the second pass when Geoff peered more closely and stiffened.

"Hold on there, mate. Cut the engine and toss out a couple of anchor chains. There's a shadow on the bottom I want to investigate."

The motor sputtered and died and the fisherman's tow-headed boy dutifully dropped anchor. My partner stepped into his fins and I helped him on with the tank. As he adjusted the straps, I swished water in his goggles to keep them from fogging and held them out for him. He stuck the breathing apparatus in his mouth and slid on the face mask. The torch was next—clipped to a strap.

"You're quite a picture," I declared approvingly. "The goateed stringbean monster near the blue lagoon. Don't frighten the fish too badly. And . . . watch out for sharks." I loaded the spear gun and handed it to him. Without saying a word he saluted, stepped over the side of the boat, and disappeared with a splash.

Both the fisherman and his young apprentice joined me as we began a vigil. The wind shifted and what I was told was a nofsinhar from Africa stirred the waves until it became difficult to keep the bucket in the water. But I did my best. The rosy coral of the reef shaded darker with every fathom. And at the base of that fossil mountain there was indeed a dark shape that looked like the outline of an ancient hulk—or at least part of it. One end was jagged as though it had been broken off. Several small fish with luminescent green stripes swam in the subdued light near the wreck. Up higher two larger sea bass nibbled at a dark patch on the coral—their silvery scales flashing colors like a prism in the sunlight. Except for Geoff beating his way downward with powerful leg kicks, that was all the life I could see. Seaweed was sparse at the bottom. Perhaps there simply wasn't enough food in the area to support a larger population. I grew even more leary of that shark attack. Only so many marauders could survive in these waters. Why had they concentrated here?

By now Geoff had reached the hulk and was swimming slowly around it—treading water every few feet to inspect or to scrape the side with the point of the spear. I was reassured by a generous column of bubbles ascending over his head. After a circuit of the ship, though, reassurance turned to waiting as my partner disappeared into the jagged hole at the end. For what seemed like an eternity, there was nothing moving around the hulk but fish. I remembered stories of giant clams, collapsing beams, and a hundred other disasters. But then Geoff emerged from inside the hull and began swimming rapidly toward us. As soon as he broke the surface, the captain and I grabbed his arms and hauled him aboard.

"Well," I asked urgently, "what did you find down there?"

Weston pulled out his mouthpiece and started unstrapping.

"I rediscovered, John, a most enjoyable past-time. I believe I shall take this equipment home with us so that on weekends—"

"What of the wreck, man!" I cut in impatiently. "Was there any treasure?"

"Oh, that." He removed a flipper. "Actually it seems to be a grain hauler—oh, perhaps two hundred feet long. The back third is missing. Probably broke up while the ship was wedged on the reef."

"Then there was nothing of value."

"I wouldn't say that. The ship itself is very old. From the way the stub of the mainmast is set far forward, I'd say it was a Roman vessel. The problem, of course, would be to raise her without breaking everything to pieces. There's a thin coating of coral on the surfaces which has preserved the wood to some extent, but I'd hate to be the one to lift her."

"Then," I concluded, "we're back where we started with no clue as to who killed Drummond."

Geoffrey unzipped his suit.

"Not at all, John. Not at all! I now know who the murderer is. The problem is going to be proving it."

"You do! Who, may I ask—"

"All in good time," Weston interrupted. "Right now I'd sooner not say anything. Premature mention of theories has already endangered one man. Let's return to the hotel to settle accounts and retrieve our bag. That should leave just time for a relaxed meal at a sidewalk cafe before we board the plane for London." He turned to the fisherman, who had overheard us and was busy raising anchor. "Captain, take us back to Valletta just as fast as this boat will travel. I'll pay for any extra petrol you use."

*   *   *   *   *

As our jet sped across France toward the English Channel, I was too excited to sleep but too tired to really think. Now that adventure gave way to routine travel and the kindly attention offered by stewardesses, it became harder to fight off fatigue. Even the snacks handed to me seemed tasteless. Geoff, on the other hand, had the annex plans out again and was scrutinizing them with the utmost care. I've never seen so much reserve energy bottled up in one man. When he's onto the scent he becomes positively tireless. I was just beginning to doze when his exclamation jerked me awake.

"How stupid of me! Of course! John, look here."

He nudged my shoulder and pointed to Twigg's simplified floor plan.

"We were lining up the Victoria Room, the painting, the door. But notice the bathroom by the side entrance. That's where Drummond was heading—not to the exit!"

"How nice," I managed with all the enthusiasm I could muster. "No doubt he cut his hand and wanted to wash off the blood."

"Taylor, don't be dense. Our problem is that we've been looking for unusual, abnormal ways out of that building. We completely overlooked the usual, expected, DESIGNED way to remove objects. Sam Drummond flushed the jewels down the toilet!"

I considered for a moment.

"That sounds plausible—providing, of course, there was some recovery system. I take it we'll be heading for the city planning office when we land."

"We will, indeed." Geoff leaned over to peer through the window. "And we shouldn't have long to wait. Unless I'm very much mistaken, that's the Strait of Dover up ahead."

Judging from the popping in my ears, our pilot had already begun a gradual descent toward London. We rushed high above water, then crossed over the cliffs of Dover. A moment later the skyline of our beloved city came into view. As we began our approach I could make out stately old Tower Bridge, the Houses of Parliament, and even Fishmongers' Hall. Then we were too low to see anything much—whizzing toward one of Heathrow's many runways.

After landing, we were subjected to an unusually long delay at customs. There was the problem of the scuba tanks. Could we open them for inspection? Not without a blow torch. Didn't we realize that their x-ray machines weren't terribly efficient in penetrating that thickness of metal? No, we could not simply leave the tanks behind.

Possible smugglers could not be allowed to walk away so easily. What had we been doing in Malta? Diving for treasure! Had we found any? My, this WAS a sticky wicket! We would have to speak with the supervisor. . . . By the time we'd unraveled the mess, it was quarter to five—far too late for us to battle rush hour traffic and arrive at the planning office before closing. Weston and I walked out of the main terminal building lugging the diving gear, an overnight bag, and a full load of exasperation toward the parking lot.

"Perhaps," I considered, "if you took the underground there'd be a chance."

"It's worth a try," Geoff agreed. "Drop me off at the Hounslow West station. Then toddle on home and get some sleep. If I find any leads to follow, I'll hail a cab."

# CHAPTER 7

## *The Hidden Reef*

Soft blackness enveloped everything. I was floating lazily in a tranquil, endless sea. But then a hollow clanging reverberated around me and sucked me relentlessly upward with ever increasing speed toward the surface. My head broke through at last and I opened my eyes. I was lying in a bed wet with my own perspiration. However, it wasn't the heat that had awakened me.

Something was wrong. But what? I felt around for my pillow only to discover that it had fallen to the floor. I'd have to turn on the lights to find it. Then I heard the sound again—this time undistorted by sleep. The doorbell rang.

"Just a moment!"

I jumped out of bed, located my robe, and hurried down the hall to the living room. The bell sounded again. I switched on the lights and glanced at the wall clock.

"Have a little patience! You can't expect instant hospitality at one in the morning!"

Evidently our caller did, however. The bell rang yet again as I pressed the gate release and opened the front door a crack. By the light of the porch lamp I could see that the man approaching with a shovel over his shoulder was not our run-of-the-mill visitor. I recognized him.

"Geoffrey! What, pray tell, have you been into? And what's that awful smell!"

My partner tried to wipe mud off his face as he stepped onto the stoop and dropped both the shovel and a foot-wide grating.

"You sound like my mother," he grinned weakly. "Actually, it's a mixture of mud and sewage. And I've just developed an intense dislike for commercial television."

"Step out of those shoes and socks," I ordered. "We'll talk after you've had a bath and I've disposed of your clothes."

"With pleasure!" He left sludge-encrusted footwear on the porch and strode past me. "I'll empty the pockets and dump what's left outside the bathroom door. If you'll get my pajamas and robe for me, I would appreciate it."

"Certainly," I agreed. "And I'll brew up some tea. You look like you could use a little refreshment."

Weston started down the hall in his bare feet.

"It's moments like these," he muttered, "that make me appreciate the promise that depth can't separate us from God's love."

He walked into the bathroom and slammed the door. Pipes groaned as the water was turned on. In a moment the door opened again and a slimy bundle fell in a heap on the carpet.

After a quick trip to the garbage can, I washed up and put a pot on the cooker. While it was heating, there was plenty of time to hang my partner's fresh wardrobe on the doorknob and pour a pail of sudsy water over the front porch. Tea and muffins sat steaming on the table when Geoffrey finally emerged. He seemed to be in considerably better spirits.

"Have a seat," I offered. "And tell me all about it."

Geoff sank wearily into the chair and took a sip from his cup.

"Thank you, John. This really hits the spot. Actually, there's not all that much to tell. I got to the planning office on time and procured a map. But I decided to visit stores and make a couple of personal visits to get background on our murderer before doing any digging. It wasn't until about nine that I arrived at the museum. Did you know there's a small park about three blocks away? Since the sewer pipes ran under it, that seemed like a likely place to start. It jolly well was! There was a flower garden in the middle of it that didn't contain any flowers at all—just freshly tilled, slightly smelly earth. It took over an hour of shoveling to get down to the pipe. When I did, I found a piece of plywood over a hole cut in the top. That grating on the front porch was still jammed into the hole.

Drummond must have put the diamonds in plastic bags and inflated them with enough air so that they were pushed along like bubbles. When they reached the grating, they were too large to pass through and an accomplice plucked them up."

I took a bite out of my muffin.

"Ingenious," I admitted. "But what's this about commercial television?"

"I should have known better," Weston admitted sheepishly. "I've read of the problem in large American cities, but it never dawned on me we were that regimented yet. The ITV network must have run a commercial, and several hundred viewers in the area all rushed to the lavatory at the same time. The hole was half full before I could scamper out. Then I had to wait until the level went down in order to replace the board and fill in the ditch. To top it all off, I was too filthy to take public transportation so I had to walk home. And when I got here, my keys weren't in my pockets."

"That," I commiserated, "is not an enjoyable series of events. But after we finish snacking, you can sleep until noon and put it behind you."

"I wish I could." Geoff drank deeply from his tea. "But unfortunately I had a little talk with Twigg earlier tonight. At eight a.m. he will have quite an assortment of people waiting for us on the bridge of the King Richard. Our job will be to unmask the killer."

"Then," I concluded, "eat quickly and get as much sleep as you can. I'm feeling rather chipper right now, myself, so it won't be any bother for me to clean up the grating and gather together the evidence envelopes."

Weston heaped marmalade onto his muffin.

"I appreciate that, John. You might also spend some time in prayer for the murderer. I really pity him."

\* \* \* \* \*

The following morning our Mercedes wended its way yet again toward the London docks. Music on the radio was interspersed with traffic reports and we navigated two successful diversions to avoid congestion. Wispy clouds overhead were giving way to thunderheads. There was a feeling in the air of impending rain—a welcome change after months of drought. I craned my neck for a better look upward.

"We could have used a few showers earlier this week," I complained. "It hasn't been much fun traipsing across half of London."

"It most assuredly hasn't," Geoff echoed, "but I rather fancy our weather has been providential."

"Providential?"

"Yes. Without it I might never have suspected the murderer. The Lord hasn't supplied us with heavenly loaded dice, but He's certainly easing us toward the criminal in other ways."

"If you say so," I remarked. "I suppose I'll find them out in a few moments."

Weston steered onto the access road to the piers. The King Richard was three berths ahead.

"I sincerely hope so," he worried. "Right now I only have enough proof to convincingly solve half the thefts and half the killings. Look, we have a welcoming party."

We certainly did. Twigg was waiting by the curb next to that old loiterer, Peterson. And the Inspector didn't look happy. My partner coasted the station wagon to a stop alongside them, and we hopped out. Weston grabbed the valise from the back seat and turned to face the detectives.

"Gentlemen," he declared solemnly, "I'm indebted to you for your cooperation. Were you able to get everyone?"

"They're here," Twigg frowned. "And this had better be good. Two of the chaps we 'invited' are only remotely connected with the case. One's your own client! If you try your usual theatrics and foul up, I warn you there will be repercussions."

"Thank you," Weston replied, "for your wholehearted confidence." There was an irrepressible twinkle in his eye. "May I suggest then we adjourn immediately to the bridge for those irresponsible pyrotechnics."

"They'd better not be," Peterson chimed in. He was a little younger and thinner than the Inspector, but just as much a stickler for decorum. "I've had a taste of your humor, and if you use tactics anything like that—"

"I assure you," Geoff interrupted, "I won't shine a light in anyone's eyes. Now let's go." He started toward the pier. "The bottom's liable to rust out of that ship before we get aboard."

That didn't happen, of course. Soon we were standing at the top of the stairs on the well-guarded second deck. I could see our "guests" through large windows designed to give the captain a good view of the sea. The skipper was indeed inside—sitting stoic and unwilling by the far wall. I could tell he was scowling at the crew from under his beard. Andrew Cook was there. So was Sir Thomas, accompanied by what looked to be his wife. And, as Twigg had predicted, Donald Wiggens, our elderly client, was very much in evidence. The fellow—never one to sit still—was in animated conversation with the cook. No doubt they were exchanging recipes. Weston pushed the hatch open and we strode into the room. All eyes turned in our direction and conversation died. Twigg—long accustomed to taking charge—stepped out front to do the introductions.

"Ladies and gentlemen." He cleared his throat. "We are all aware of the seriousness of crimes recently committed. A sailor on this ship has been cunningly murdered, and some priceless diamonds are missing. I've arranged this meeting because . . . well, frankly, we would like to bring matters to a conclusion while there's still an outside chance at recovering the jewels intact. Mr. Weston, whom I admire in spite of occasional differences of opinion, feels that one of you is a thief and a murderer. And we now propose to determine which one it is. Geoff, the floor's all yours."

The Inspector settled back into an easy chair. Both Peterson and I followed his example—leaving Weston to face the crowd. My partner stood for a moment with his hands behind his back surveying the cabin. The top of his head nearly touched the ceiling.

"Thank you, Inspector." He sniffed the air and glanced toward a large burn mark scarring the redness of the carpet. "But I'm not sure I want the floor. It seems to have been treated rather carelessly of late."

Tiny Stedders and the two machinists burst out laughing—remembering the pipe incident. Cosgrove glared at them with undisguised hatred. My partner began pacing.

"Actually," he continued in a more serious vein, "this case is far more complex than even Twigg realizes. It involves two murders, not one. Wally, did any garbage disappear from the galley the day before O'Brian was attacked?"

"I don't rightly know." The cook bit his lip. "But I seem to remember going one extra day before having ta empty the pail."

Weston nodded thoughtfully.

"I suspected as much. Someone tossed garbage overboard to attract sharks to the area."

"But," the captain objected sourly, "that doesn't mean they'd attack Skinny—even if the stuff was dumped right around him. And it wasn't. That would have been a bloomin' impossibility."

"It probably would," Geoff agreed. He stooped down for his briefcase, laid it flat on a table, and opened the lid slightly to extract a jar. "But you'll notice this container of bouillon." He held it up for all to see. "There's one identical but almost empty container in Drummond's cabin.

I'm virtually certain that Sam made a paste of the stuff and smeared it in the space between O'Brian's scuba tanks where it wouldn't be detected. During the night the soup dried to a hard, odorless cake. But as soon as Skinny jumped in the water it began dissolving again—leaving a trail as tantalizing as blood for the sharks to follow."

"That's absolutely horrid!" Mrs. Dodd shuddered, tossing her chestnut hair over her shoulders.

"If it happened," Dodd added skeptically. "But this all sounds like mere conjecture."

Geoff ignored the comment and addressed the first mate.

"Tiny, did you ever see Drummond drink bouillon?"

"Only at mess, and then 'e wasn't 'appy about it. Claimed Cosgrove was too cheap to buy decent soup."

"Now see here!" The captain jumped to his feet. "I got a belly full of insults last night and—"

"Sit down!" Twigg shouted, "or you'll get a belly full of gaol tonight."

The captain returned reluctantly to his seat. He clearly wished he were anyplace else on earth—almost.

"Thank you." Weston nodded in appreciation to the Inspector. "Now you are all probably wondering what difference it makes whether Skinny was murdered or not—since the murderer has himself been killed."

Sir Thomas crossed his legs.

"The idea had been banging about in my brain," he commented dryly. "I assume you see some sort of pattern in the deaths."

"More than that," Weston corrected—eyeing each of the suspects. "I don't believe Drummond thought up the scheme for killing the other diver. He didn't seem to be a particularly imaginative chap. It's far more likely he was acting under the orders of a confederate—the same one who helped him steal the Weatherford collection."

"By George, you've done it again!" Lady Dodd gasped. "You keep telling my husband how much you believe in him. You've even preached him into making some strange religious 'decision' in gaol. But every time you open your mouth he's suspected of another crime! You're a despicable—"

"Now, Caroline," Sir Thomas interrupted sternly, "that outburst is uncalled for."

"Particularly," Weston added, "since you, Mrs. Dodd, are a far more likely suspect than is your husband."

"I!" She looked dully at Geoff for a second. Then her brown eyes flashed. "You . . . You ARE a scoundrel. I have no connection whatsoever with—"

"Oh, yes you do." My colleague stopped his pacing and pointed an accusing finger at her. "I read the society pages. It's you—not your husband—who has the gambling debts. You needed money. And you had access to your husband's keys. It was a simple matter, wasn't it, to make a plastic copy of one of the master keys and pass it on to Drummond? You knew about the diamonds. You knew the routine of the building through visiting your husband at work. And, Mrs. Dodd, poison is a woman's weapon."

"No!" Caroline shrieked. "It wasn't that way at all. I didn't know . . . I mean I don't know what you're talking about."

Weston held her in an icy stare.

" 'I didn't know . . . ' " he repeated. "Finish that sentence the way you intended. 'I didn't know who he was or what he was going to do with it.' "

Caroline Dodd hung her head and began weeping.

"I owed a gambler five hundred pounds," she sobbed. "And last week he threatened to kill Tommy if I didn't give him the money or a wax impression of one of. . . . So I gave him the most useless one I could find. It only fit the closets and. . . . " She sobbed uncontrollably until Sir Thomas put his arm around her and drew her close.

"One last question," Geoff went on doggedly. "Is that man in this room or did he perchance have a scar on his lip?"

She shook her head emphatically and continued crying softly.

"Then," Weston concluded, "the gambler was himself probably contacted by either Sam or his accomplice and either paid outright or offered a share in the booty. Twigg, get together with Mrs. Dodd after this session and obtain a description of the man. He shouldn't be too hard to locate." My partner turned his attention to Sir Thomas. "We have now, Dodd, reduced the number of suspects by two. Since a key was copied, you are automatically innocent of the theft. You might, of course, have learned your wife was being blackmailed and hunted Drummond down. But I think that unlikely. Even if you had, you probably would have throttled him. I can't imagine you using arsenic."

"Thank you," Sir Thomas replied in a voice dripping with sarcasm. "You've no idea how wonderful it makes me feel to know my wife will take my place in prison."

Weston met his gaze with compassion.

"I doubt she'll get more than probation," he predicted, "perhaps not even that. And it's worth that price if she stays away from the gaming tables."

Thomas Dodd patted his wife's shoulder and looked sorrowfully down at her.

"You're probably right," he admitted. "Something like this had to happen sometime."

"I'm touched by all this sentiment," Cosgrove cut in acidly. "But I've better things to do than watch silly women make fools of themselves. Get on with the show, Weston, so we can put this inquisition behind us."

My partner stroked his goatee and smiled in the shipowner's direction.

"Very well, captain. Let's discuss your involvement in the case."

"That's all right by me," Cosgrove challenged. "I've nothing to hide."

"Everyone," Geoff disagreed, "has *something* to hide. But I'm going to quite probably surprise you. In spite of the evidence, I don't believe you're guilty of murder."

" 'In spite of the evidence!' " The captain slammed a fist into his open palm. "In spite of WHAT evidence!"

"Oh," Weston remarked, "I imagine I could make a rather good case against you if I wanted. You're shrewd—shrewd enough to invent a way to get jewels out of the museum. As a matter of fact, the scheme would be a natural for a sailor. Float the diamonds out through a sewer pipe on little life preservers. Then stop them with an obstruction—a reef if you will—in the line." Geoff reached into his briefcase again and pulled out the iron grating. "This, incidentally, was the obstruction used. I dug it up last night."

"Hold on a minute," Twigg interrupted. "Where did you find it?"

"In a park three blocks south of the annex." Geoff handed the Inspector the rusty metal. "If you excavate to take a picture, please watch out for some keys I lost."

"That's not all you've lost," Cosgrove criticized. "You've lost your mind if you call any of your prattle evidence."

"Oh," my partner replied good-naturedly, "but there's more—much more. Neither of the Dodds could be connected with *both* dead men. But you can. And your greed is notorious. It's not hard to picture you conspiring with both divers to rob the museum. Then, since only one accomplice was really necessary, you might have eliminated one before the theft and the other afterwards—leaving yourself with all the money. I found some wax in Skinny's cabin. Perhaps he hit on the idea of copying the key. You had a possible motive for murder. And you certainly had opportunity. You even had a chance to plant bouillon in Drummond's cabin when you sneaked in after his death and stole his share."

"When I what!"

"Come now," Weston's face seemed cut from granite. "You *did* steal his share, you know. Your own testimony places you outside Sam's cabin just after he died—at about eight-thirty. Perhaps a few final groans were wafted on the breeze. You went in, took the money, and made two fatal mistakes."

"Which were?" Cosgrove appraised his opponent warily from behind his beard.

"You couldn't resist closing the window," Geoff explained. "The horrible smell inside might attract attention, and it would be inconvenient if the body were discovered before you'd made a regularly scheduled trip ashore with the money. In your zeal to avoid arousing suspicion, however, you aroused it. I might otherwise have assumed Drummond hid his treasure on land. But a closed porthole placed someone in his cabin after the death. Sam never would have spent a minute in that sweltering room without opening the window—if he were alive.

"You also made a mistake in where you hid the booty. Oh yes, I know where it is. After putting some thought into the matter, I realized you'd pick a spot both unlikely to be searched and unlikely to arouse suspicion of wrongdoing if it was. But, captain, can you really expect us to believe Sam would hide the bills in his own wet suit when he might have to use it for work?"

"If," Cosgrove flared, "you find any envelope in his diving gear, it wasn't me that put it there. And you can't prove otherwise."

"I might not be able to," Weston agreed solemnly, "except that I never told you the money was in an envelope. How would you know that unless you'd taken it?"

The color drained slowly from the captain's face. He was trapped and knew with a cold certainty he couldn't lie his way out.

"All right," he admitted weakly, "so I took the envelope. But all that other rot about killing the divers and taking jewels is pure bilgewater. You've got to believe that."

"Oh, I do," Geoff assured him with a smile. "If you'll remember, I told you so right at the beginning. You're a grave robber, not a murderer." He gestured toward the group. "Now let's focus our attention on someone else."

Bobby Black raised a grimy hand in protest.

"Look here, Weston. I'm beginnin' ta feel uneasy. Every chap you talk to is guilty of somethin'. Why don't you eliminate a few of us and get on to exposin' the rest."

My colleague's eyes sparkled.

"You might have a point there," he agreed.

"I've noticed some of you have been rather quiet. Reverend Cook, you haven't said a word. Neither have you, Brady. And Wiggens, you've certainly made yourself inconspicuous. I suppose I have been rather intimidating."

"It's not so much that," Andrew Cook pointed out, "as it is a lack of knowledge. I've been trying to discover what this is all about, and why I'm here. I assume that it has something to do with who was sitting in the pews or with knowledge I might have about poor Sam."

"It does indeed, Rector. But we'll get to that in a moment." Weston resumed his pacing. "There is one solid—or should I say liquid—piece of evidence which proves Cosgrove didn't kill Sam. John and I discovered a puddle of water on the floor by Drummond's sink. Interestingly enough, even accounting for evaporation, it was far too acid. And it contained a high level of photochemical oxidants. Put simply, the puddle was straight from the Thames. There's only one explanation I can think of as to how it got there. Some other diver came out of the river—probably while the crew was at mess—climbed up the side of the ship with a rope, and poisoned Sam's toothpaste. Since it took a few seconds standing in front of the sink to get the job done, a puddle collected. And since the deck was dark, Peterson couldn't see anything from the shore."

"But that," Twigg complained, "puts us right back where we started from. It clears the whole crew and starts us looking for some nameless, faceless chap that slinks out of the deep. It could be the gambler. It could be one of the guards. It could be some acquaintance in a pub who heard Sam mention his newfound riches."

"I suppose you're right," Weston admitted. "But it wasn't. I must say I've suspected for some time who the murderer was. But I couldn't fit all the pieces together until yesterday when I saw a certain sunken hulk off the coast of Malta. Gentlemen, let me share a few pertinent facts with you about that vessel. It struck a reef. The stern section was destroyed by wave action. The approach run to the reef is in water fifteen fathoms deep. There's a bay on the other side of the obstruction—a bay with a beach. The ship was a large wooden grain carrier—perhaps one thousand tons. And there were no skeletons aboard. Does all that mean anything to you?"

Donald Wiggens had taken out a note pad and was writing down particulars as though Lloyds had insured the ship. But at the question, he stopped writing and drummed his fingers against the page.

"No," he ventured thoughtfully. "Should it?"

"It should," Geoff assured him, "to someone here. You see, ladies and gentlemen, there's a famous shipwreck which exactly fits that set of particulars. Paul, on the way to Rome to stand trial before Caesar, had his ship strike a reef in Malta. The Book of Acts describes the event in detail. God promised and it came about that no one was killed. The approach run to the reef was in fifteen fathoms of water. And I could go on point by point. It is a virtual certainty that the wreck I saw yesterday *was the ship on which the Apostle Paul traveled!* That would make it quite valuable, wouldn't you say?"

"Priceless," I enthused. "And it would explain why Skinny O'Brian was killed. He must have discovered what the hulk was worth."

"That's the irony of it," Weston disagreed. "I don't think he ever knew."

Geoff stopped long enough to open the briefcase again. He took out an envelope, opened it, and held its contents for us to see.

"This lump of wax," he informed us, "was found in Skinny's room after his death. I believe it was the reason *for* his death. No, it wasn't used for making keys. My somewhat fanciful talk with Cosgrove had its weaknesses. It didn't establish much of a motive for O'Brian's murder, and it didn't really explain the wax—since Mrs. Dodd, not Skinny, was the one who used the stuff. What's more, she couldn't have passed it along to him. O'Brian was killed before Lady Dodd made the impression. That then leaves us with a rather mysterious lump. It's not Queen Victoria's toe either."

"Dispense with the levity," Twigg demanded in a peeved voice. "Get to the point."

"The point, Inspector, is that a fellow once suggested raising the Titanic by pumping hot wax into it through hoses. Wax, you know, is lighter than water. The plan was rejected as impractical because the ship had too many compartments and was too large. It would have cost a fortune to fill it up. But that method would not be at all impractical for raising the hulk in Malta. In fact, it's the *only* way the job could be done. Wax pumped into the hold would harden as soon as it hit the water—turning the ship, for all practical purposes, into one solid lump. Cut away the slight coral incrustation at the bottom and the vessel would float up like a cork without any strain on the fragile wooden hull! Skinny had the piece of wax because he was toying with the idea and testing for buoyancy. He told his friend Drummond, and in return, Drummond received instructions to kill him to keep the salvage operation from succeeding. No, John, Skinny didn't know the value of the vessel. Only one person could have known that—the person who told Sam Drummond. The person who went scuba diving, not swimming, with him. The only suspect with enough knowledge of the Bible to recognize the ship when Drummond wrote him about it . . . " Weston pointed his slim finger at the surprised cleric. "You, Andrew Cook, are the murderer!"

"But . . . but . . . " Andrew's chubby face hinted at desperation. He looked around frantically for support from some quarter. "But this is preposterous! Absolutely preposterous. I'm a man of the cloth. I have no need for money. I . . . You've no proof!"

Weston stood and watched Cook with grey steely eyes. My partner's next words were deliberate and chilling.

"You, sir, are a scoundrel. It wasn't self-sacrifice I saw when I visited. It was poverty seething in discontentment, pride, and greed. We talked then about Heidegger and Bultmann and their form of criticism. But we should have discussed one of their other views—the idea that a man must escape the depersonalized crowd and authenticate himself by doing something decisive. You swallowed that concept hook, line and sinker, didn't you?" Geoff shook his head in disgust. "And it didn't make any difference to you whether that something was extremely good or outrageously evil. Just as long as it made you rich and famous! That's all you cared about."

"Stop it!" Cook bounced out of the chair livid with rage—a short, fat bantam rooster ready to do battle. "You're telling lies!" he shouted. "Lies!"

"My, my," Weston scolded. "We seem to have let our hypocritical guard down to reveal a temper."

"You . . . " the rector sputtered, "you'd be angry too if someone accused you of murder." He fought to control himself—realizing he was hurting his own cause. With an effort of will he sank back into his seat.

"Actually," Geoff amended, "I'm accusing you of more than murder. I'm accusing you of spiritual blindness and outright stupidity. When you realized Sam had found the Apostle Paul's ship, you should have fallen on your knees and begged God to forgive you for doubting the historical accuracy of His book. Then you jolly well should have thrown your library in the garbage.

But did you do that? No. Instead you began scheming to make your church famous and to gain a larger audience for your own feeble thoughts. The ship would look nice on the lawn next to your church, wouldn't it? St. Albans would become a shrine. People would come from all over the world to see it and make donations. Eventually you could build a new church right around the vessel. And all you had to do to authenticate yourself in that way was have Sam kill his friend, rob the British Museum for operating capital, and raise the ship. Of course, in the end you also had to kill Drummond when you realized from your conversation with me that I knew about the payoff. Sam, poor chap, was the weak link and had to be eliminated."

By now Andrew was in complete possession of his temper. He'd crossed his legs, lit a cigarette, and was smirking between puffs.

"Please excuse my outburst, gentlemen." He addressed Twigg. "Inspector, certainly you can't take this man's ravings seriously. All he's done is make unfounded charges about some boat I've never heard of before today. He offers no evidence, only farfetched fairy tales."

Twigg, who had been taking notes of his own, put the tip of the pen in his mouth and considered a moment before answering.

"I would say," he observed shrewdly, "that Weston has hard evidence in reserve or he wouldn't have made the accusations. You, sir, are in need of a couple of alibis."

"That's tellin' 'im," Tiny joined in. "What I seen today's amazin', and I wouldn't give a tuppence for yer chances."

Andrew glared at the mate.

"Why you—"

"That will be enough," Geoff interrupted. "As a matter of fact, Reverend, I *have* come across a few incriminating oddities that you might wish to explain. When we first met you—right after church—you had just finished polishing your shoes. Now I could understand that if it were raining outside. You might have gotten them soiled on your way across the lawn from the rectory. But a drop hasn't fallen in weeks. And nobody polishes shoes *after* church in dry weather. What then should we conclude? By your own admission you have but one pair of shoes. The answer seems rather obvious to me. The previous afternoon you were out digging in a park near the museum. You got your footwear and trousers rather soiled. But there wasn't time for more than a perfunctory hosing down before making the rounds to the fences. You sold a few diamonds—but not many. And you reached home late. The shoes required a second cleaning and, therefore, were not dry by the time the service started. Or perhaps you overslept. At any rate you couldn't polish them until just before we arrived."

"That sounds very ingenious," Cook smiled. "But as it happens, I scuffed them on a step. You're building a skyscraper out of toothpicks."

"Am I now?" Geoff declared seriously. "May I see those shoes, please?"

The rector's smile faltered and the confidence faded from his eyes.

"What do you want them for?"

"Simply give them to me," Weston repeated. "You'll find out."

"I'm sure of that," he spat with distrust. "But they're *my* shoes."

Geoff shrugged.

"Have it your way. Twigg can remove them after the arrest. When he does I'm sure the Yard's laboratory will detect traces of a most unusual mixture of mud and sewage in the cracks under the polish. Then, of course, there's the question of the poison. With a large empty building like you have, I imagine you use quite a bit to keep the rats under control, don't you? As a matter of fact, the poison register at the Seaside Apothecary, only a few blocks from your home, shows such a purchase only two months ago. Arsenic, I believe it was. How do you explain that?"

Andrew Cook was no longer the jolly public-relations-oriented pastor. And his cheeks had lost the rosiness we'd seen in our first meeting. But he maintained a cold, dead sort of composure.

"I'm not going to say another word to you," he decided. "If you have any questions, you can speak with my lawyer."

"A wise move," Geoff agreed. "Twigg, he's all yours."

"Thanks so much for the honor," the Inspector scowled. He unlimbered himself from his chair and surveyed the cabin from its brass fittings and plush carpet to the windows—behind which bobbies stood on duty. At length his gaze rested on the Dodds. "I don't believe it would be irregular, Sir Thomas, for me to remand Lady Caroline to your custody. Bring her to the Yard this afternoon to sign a statement and give us a full description of the gambler. You will be told at a later date when to appear in court. I'm confident you have enough roots so you won't be running off anywhere."

Thomas Dodd, his arm still around his wife, looked up gratefully at the Inspector.

"That's very kind of you, sir." His voice broke. "Rest assured we'll be there."

"I'm sure you will." Twigg now shifted his attention to Captain Cosgrove and Reverend Cook. "As for you two gentlemen, please consider yourselves under arrest. And do come peacefully. There are enough officers outside this room so that any attempt to escape will most surely result in a broken arm." He signaled and reinforcements came in through the door.

# *Epilogue*

That afternoon Geoff, Donald Wiggens, and I sat before an elegantly covered table stacked with stuffed pheasant, shrimp salad, and a hundred different forks. Our client had invited us out to celebrate!

"This artichoke soup is scrumptious," I remarked above the clanking of plates and the background conversation. "I hope Twigg arrives in time to enjoy some while it's hot."

"Don't worry." Weston took a bite of stuffing. "I've never known Filbert to pass up a free meal. When he comes, perhaps he'll have word on the search of St. Albans. That really *could* give us something to celebrate."

Donald Wiggens, as dapper as ever in a blue suit, adjusted the napkin on his lap.

"Mr. Weston, I have an apology to make. This morning you did a rattling good job. But for a while there, I actually thought I was a suspect. Please forgive me for doubting you."

"There are no apologies necessary, old chap." Geoff smiled disarmingly. "You *were* one. After all, you'd made a study of the security system. You could have discovered the flaw, stolen the jewels, and hired me as a diversion. But you weren't, I'll admit, a very high priority suspect."

"There's one detail of the case," I confessed, "that still confuses me. Why did Drummond try to burn the key on the spot instead of just dropping it down the toilet with the diamonds?"

Geoff gestured with a forkful of pheasant.

"Now that's one of the more interesting aspects of the crime. There was no reason for *him* to burn it. But *Andrew* had everything to gain from the procedure. That way if Drummond were caught carrying the jewels to the lavatory, the secret of the key would still be safe and the rector could try again. The burned key told me Sam was only following orders."

"I can't understand a man like Cook," our grey-haired host admitted. "As many years as I've lived I've never met a preacher like that."

"There's not much mystery to it," I pointed out. "The book of Jude tells about men who are hidden reefs in the Christians' love feasts. And he was a reef in more ways than one."

Geoff drank deeply from a glass of tomato juice he'd ordered in place of bouillon.

"I think I'd prefer a shark simile," he suggested. "The fellow was ravenous, deadly, and totally empty. No matter how many men he devoured, the hunger pangs never slackened. He must be terribly unhappy. Let's hope he follows Sir Thomas' example and becomes a real Christian while behind bars. I'll be praying to that end."

"Look over there," I directed. "Here comes Twigg grinning like the Cheshire cat. I'll bet he found the diamonds."

My companions looked over just in time to catch sight of the Inspector wending his way toward us. As we watched he squeezed between the last two tables, came over and sat down with an immense sigh of contentment.

"Sorry I'm late, chaps. But while men of leisure dine, the rest of us have to work."

"You'll love the gooseberry sauce," I advised. "Did you find them?"

Twigg unbuttoned his coat, then pulled his chair closer to the table.

"Of course," he declared expansively. "Almost the entire collection was in the church basement. We also found a hibachi that fits the grating—or is it the other way around? That blighter Cook's a hypocrite to the end, though. Claims Drummond put the stuff there. Wait until we get back the analysis of those shoes!"

"I'm glad matters have been resolved quickly," I beamed. "Geoff and I have reservations for an evening flight to Mexico."

"Business or pleasure?" Twigg asked as he lifted the fork to his mouth.

"Business," Weston admitted. "The President's son just sent us a telegram. As nearly as I can make out the Spanish, someone stole his shadow."

"Sounds like a bloomin' Peter Pan!" Wiggens injected.

"Doesn't it though?" the Inspector agreed between chews. "But I'm sure you'll get to the root of the matter. Your use of logic in this last case was impressive, Geoff, and I don't mind saying so. I should have suspected the drain pipes when that bulky necklace was left behind. But the rest of the mystery was beyond me."

"It wouldn't have been," Weston teased, "if you had read your Bible."

"As a matter of fact," I added seriously, "we've got six hours before our plane leaves. That's plenty of time for the four of us to study through the Book of Acts. As a policeman, Twigg, you should be fascinated by the Philippian jailor."